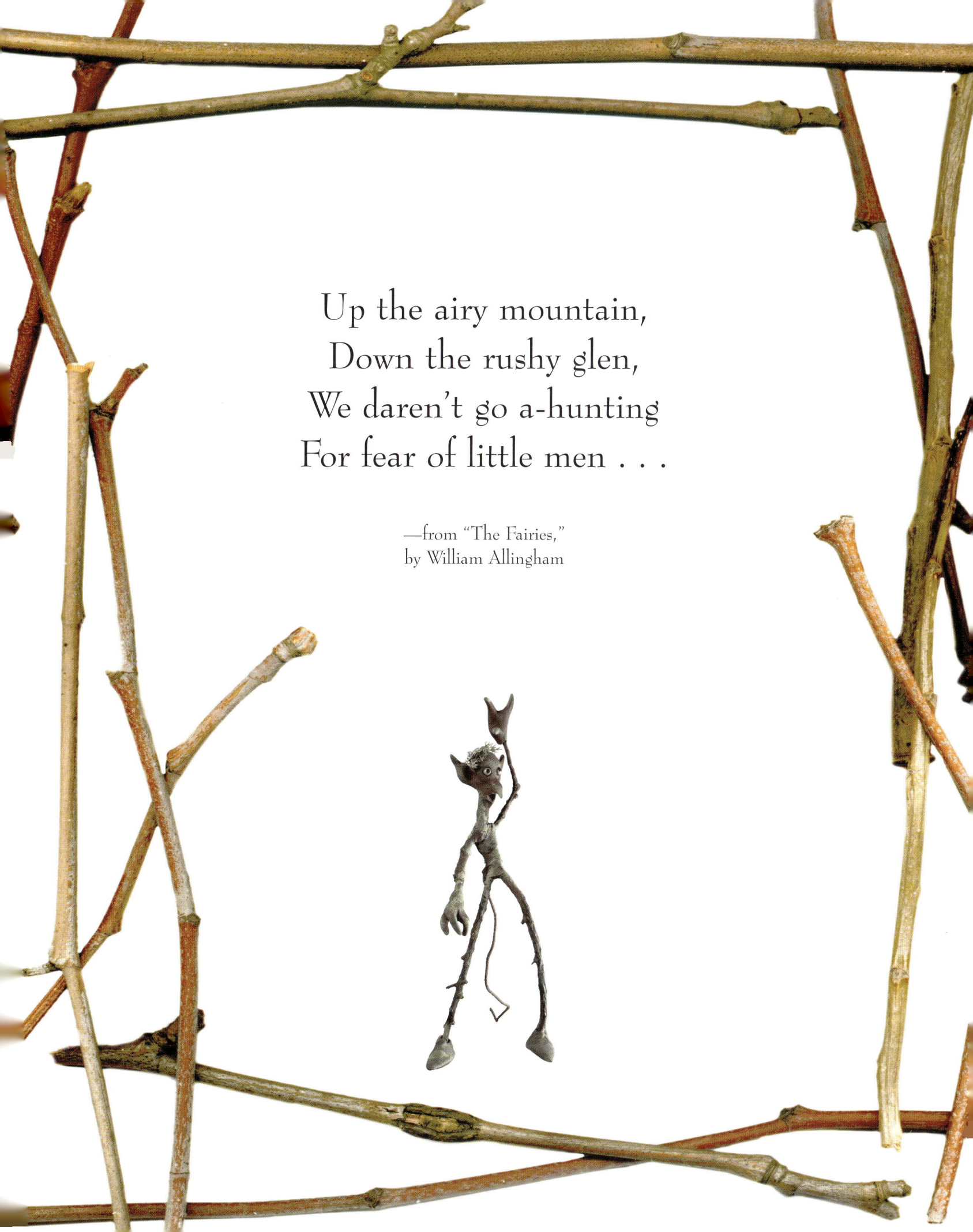

Up the airy mountain,
Down the rushy glen,
We daren't go a-hunting
For fear of little men . . .

—from "The Fairies,"
by William Allingham

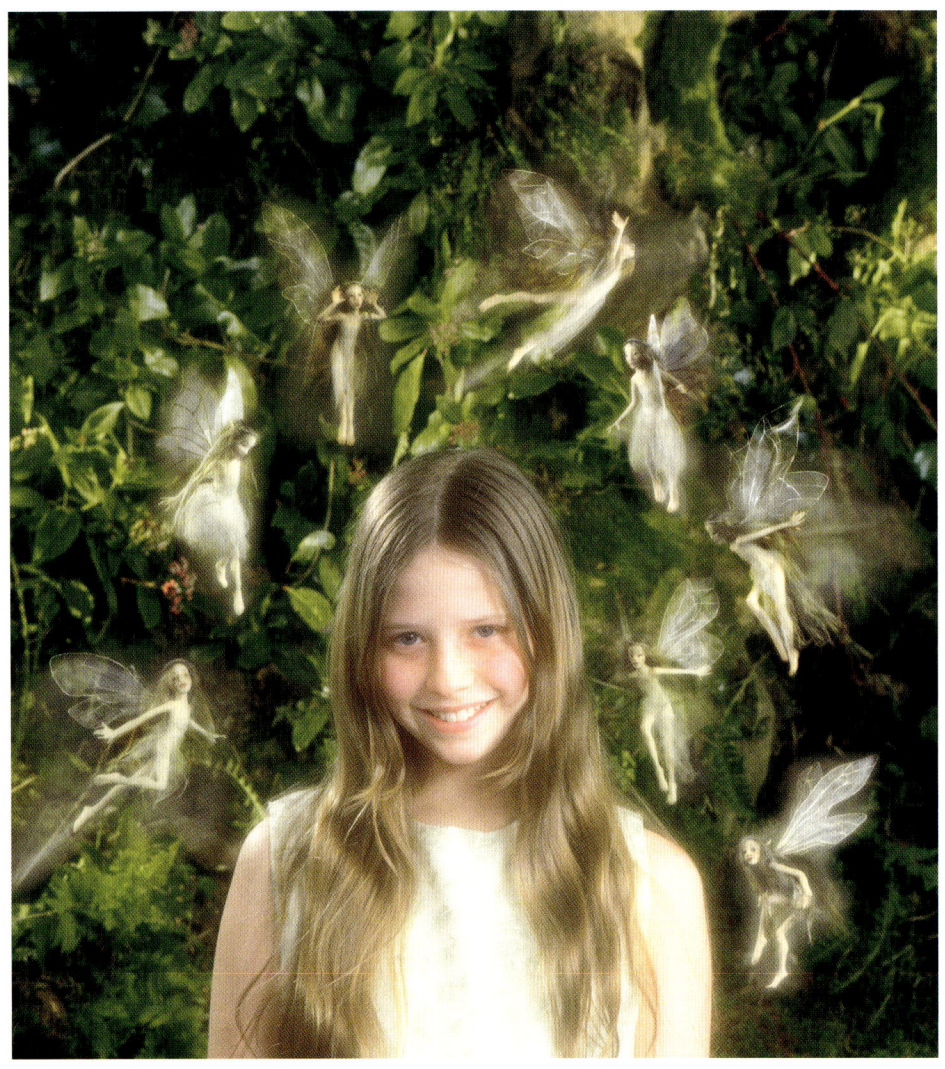

This book is for Toby, Lillian, David, and Elynor, with our love.
—Wendy Froud and Terri Windling

Books from the World of Froud: *The Winter Child* by Wendy Froud and Terri Windling
A Midsummer Night's Faery Tale by Wendy Froud and Terri Windling • *The Faeries' Oracle* by Brian Froud; text by Jessica Macbeth
Good Faeries, Bad Faeries by Brian Froud; edited by Terri Windling
Strange Stains and Mysterious Smells by Brian Froud; text by Terry Jones
Visit the official Brian and Wendy Froud website: www.worldoffroud.com

Books by Terri Windling: *My Swan Sister and Other Retold Fairy Tales* (edited with Ellen Datlow) • *The Wood Wife*
The Raven Queen (with Ellen Steiber) • *The Green Man: Tales from the Mythic Forest* (edited with Ellen Datlow)
Black Heart, Ivory Bones (edited with Ellen Datlow) • *A Wolf at the Door* (edited with Ellen Datlow)
Visit Terri Windling's Endicott Studio of Mythic Arts: www.endicott-studio.com

ACKNOWLEDGMENTS

Wendy would like to thank Brian for a wonderful job of art direction, set design, and building; John Lawrence Jones for beautiful photographs; Simon Terrey for post production; Lillian Todd Jones for modeling; Robert Gould for all of his help and encouragement; literary agent Muriel Nellis; and Guy, Todd, and Carol for constant support.
Terri would like to second all of the above, and add thanks to editors Constance Herndon and Amanda Murray for their aid with the story from proposal to finished draft; to her agent Christopher Schelling and to Delia Sherman for astute editorial advice; to Ellen Kushner and Richard and Mardelle Kunz for constant support; and to Miko, who was a prince indeed, for the use of his name

The Faeries of Spring Cottage

Art by Wendy Froud

Story by Terri Windling

Photographs by John Lawrence Jones

Sets and Photographic Art Direction by Brian Froud

Simon & Schuster
New York   London   Toronto   Sydney   Singapore

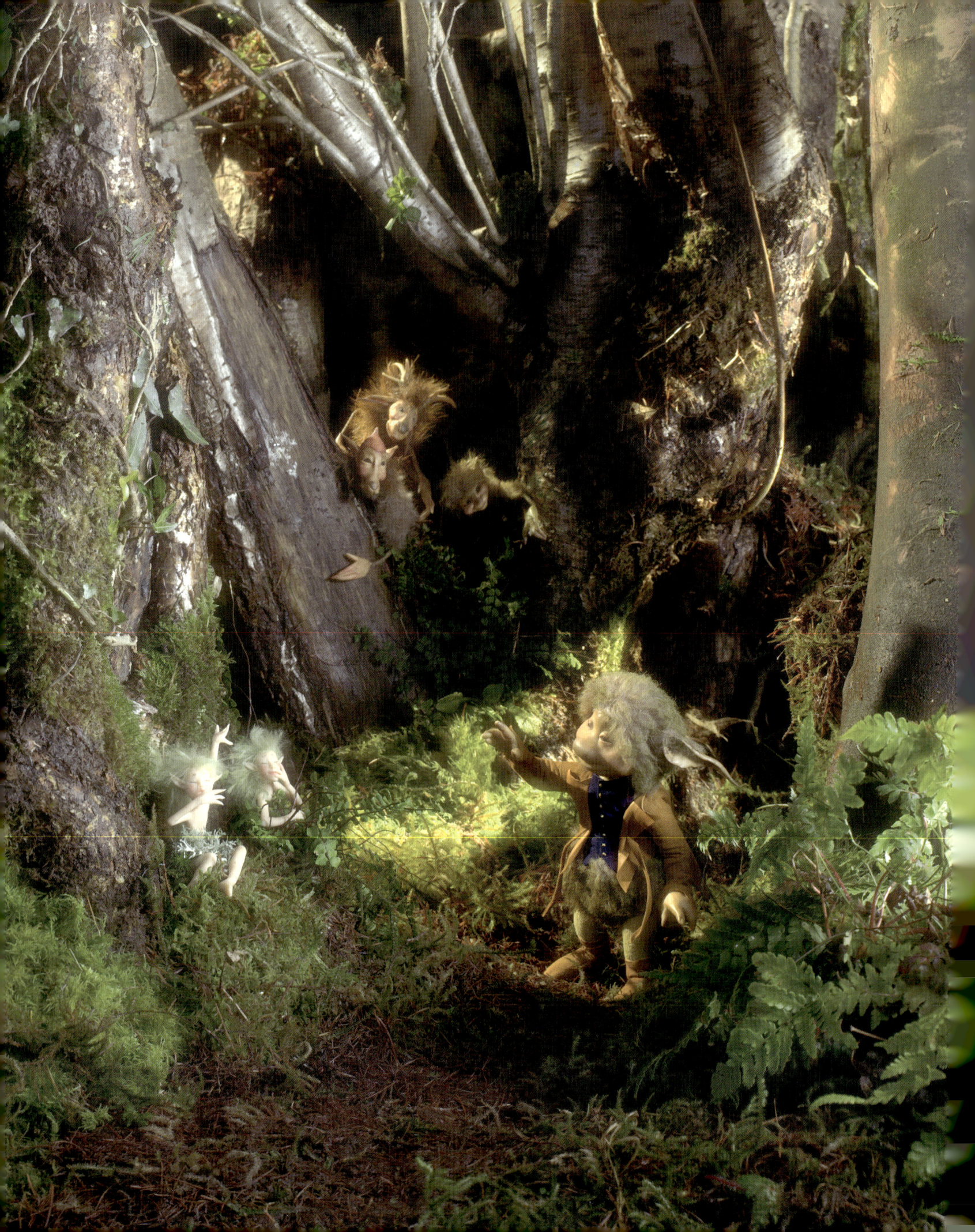

When Sneezlewort Rootmuster Rowanberry Boggs the Seventh woke up one fine spring morning, he stepped outside the door of his tiny stone house into the light of the day, never guessing that this might be the last time he ever saw home again.

He followed a wandering path through crooked oaks that were as old as time—for Old Oak Wood was a magical forest hidden deep in moorland hills, home to the oldest faery court in all the British Isles. Sneezle himself was a tree root faery, but merely a child in faery years—although he was now 201 as humans reckon time. He came from a fine old hawthorn clan, and like every other Boggs in the woods he had nut-brown fur, black eyes, long ears, and a tail he was exceedingly proud of.

On that particular April morning, the young root faery followed his nose until he reached the bank of a chattering stream, where the path turned south. Overhead, the oak trees yawned and stretched away their winter dreams. Likewise, the hibernating faeries—the hobs, the nobs, piskies and pooks—were waking now, crawling from their dens beneath the rocks and roots to blink up at the sun, their faces pale, still half asleep.

The boy followed the stream through the morning hours until the sun was high, whereupon he reached a tranquil pool shaded by an elder tree. A dryad sat beneath the tree, her skin the color of elder wood, the long braids of her hair trailing in the dark water below.

The young root faery cleared his throat and said, "Good day to you, Lady."

The dryad turned and gazed at him with eyes as pale as elder wine. "Good day to you, small one," she said, her voice the rustle of leaves in the wind. She was just as ancient as her tree, her features carved by weather and time, grown ever more beautiful with age. Sneezle bowed before her.

"I've come to ask if you will spare some elder sticks for my friend Twig. She's studying magic," Sneezle explained, "and she needs them for her spells."

The elder dryad's eyes narrowed. "And what shall you give to me in return?"

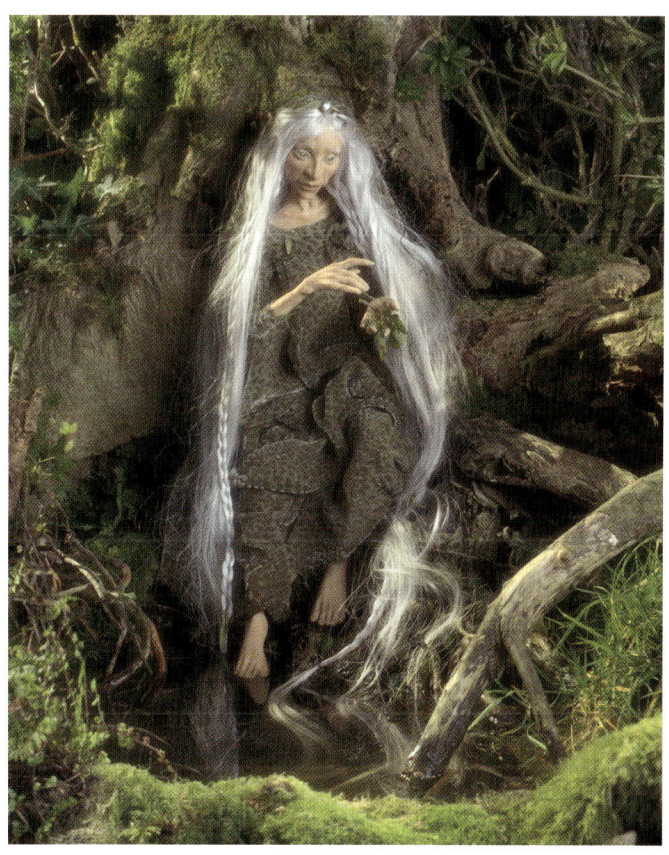

"I'll give you a story," said Sneezle promptly, for this was what dryads loved best.

The woman frowned. "My tree was old when yours was just a seed," she said. "What story can you possibly know that will interest one such as me?"

"I'll tell you about the Winter Child born from a golden egg," said the boy, "and how I rescued her from a goblin tower with my friend Twig."

The dryad favored him with a smile. "Then you must be young Sneezlewort Boggs."

"I am, Lady," he answered, surprised.

"The trees have spoken of you, small one. Come sit beside me, tell me your tale, and I'll give you something better than sticks. I'll give you twigs from the very top of the tree, where the magic is."

Sneezle sat down on gray rocks, his legs dangling above the pool, and told the elder dryad the entire story of his last adventure. The telling took a long, long time, and when he'd finished the tale at last, the clear blue sky had changed to one that promised rain by evening. Eager to be indoors by then, Sneezle said farewell to the tree woman, elder twigs tucked safely into the pocket of his waistcoat.

Before he'd traveled far, however, the sky darkened alarmingly, and Sneezle knew he'd never make it home before the rain. And so he searched the woods for a rabbit hole or the hollow of a tree where he could wait, cozy and dry, until the storm had passed. This was unfamiliar territory, close to the woodland's edge. Through thinning trees he could glimpse the open moor that lay beyond it. Like all root faeries, the misty land outside the forest frightened him. Its bleak, barren, treeless hills, populated by sheep and standing stones, seemed vast and terrifying compared to the green world of the forest.

Humans lived out there, and human beings could be quite dangerous—especially the ones who did not believe in elfinkind. Nestled within the rolling hills he could see a distant human dwelling: a solitary cottage made of stone, with a roof of thatch. Sneezle himself had never seen a human. Perhaps he never would. His uncle Starbucket said that they looked like giants and smelled like fish.

The boy felt a single drop of rain. Storm clouds filled the sky above. He hurried on until he found a hollow in a fallen oak. From the safety of his hiding place, he watched as winged faeries flew past, buffeted by the gusting wind as they, too, looked for shelter. Two rabbits bounded down the path. Then a beak-nosed brownie passed, followed by a tiny foxglove faery, eyes wide with terror.

The foxglove faery was running from six pursuers—six tattered little men. They cornered her among the tree roots, brandishing swords and pikes. These odd creatures weren't faeries themselves; they weren't goblins or Big People. They were nothing Sneezle had ever seen before, or even heard of. Their long limbs looked like knobby sticks, their wicked teeth were as sharp as thorns, their clothes were formed of leaves and bark and their hair of matted weeds.

The foxglove faery cried out pitifully. The little men advanced, teeth and eyes glinting, as the faery sank down to her knees.

"Hey, you there!" cried Sneezle, leaping from his hiding place. "Leave her alone!"

The tattered creatures turned, growling. The foxglove faery darted away, forgotten by the little men as they pounced on a better prize.

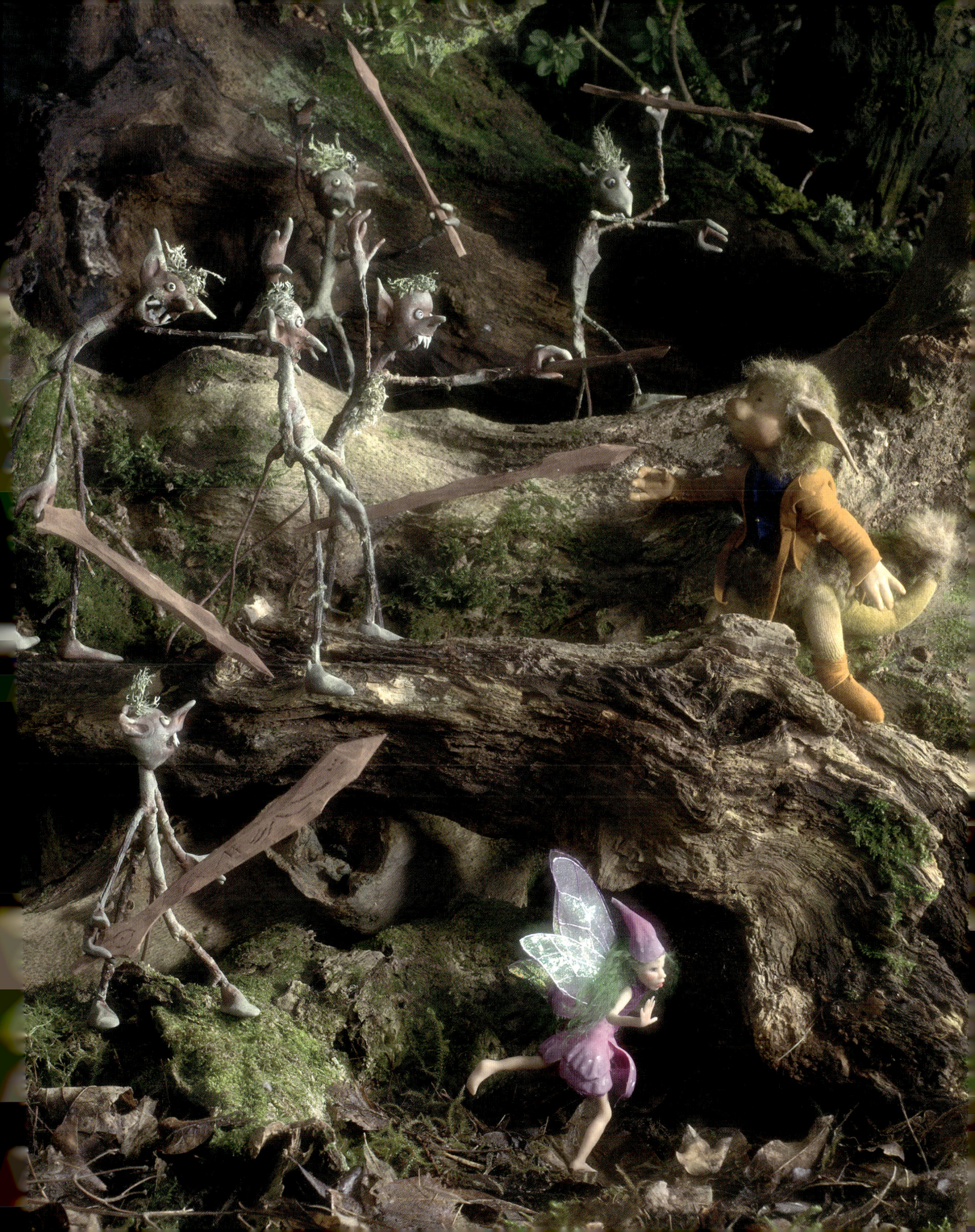

Sneezle whirled to flee, tripped over roots, and fell to the stony ground. A knobby hand grabbed at his foot. He flailed and kicked the hand away just as another creature raised a crude sword high above him. The swordsman smiled nastily, exposing all his terrible teeth. Then thunder cracked above them and the rain began to fall.

The growling of the little men turned into shrieks beneath the rain, and the sword poised over Sneezle's head fell harmlessly to the ground. The horrid creatures hissed and steamed as rain fell on their flesh, their clothes . . . and then the little men *dissolved,* as Sneezle gaped in wonder. Soon, all that was left of them were lumps of mud, leaf mulch, and twigs . . . a pile of wooden swords and pikes . . . and one dirty knitted cap.

The young root faery got back to his feet, panting, splattered with mud, and stared down at the rain-sodden remains of the vicious creatures. He picked a sword up from the pile, looked it over curiously, then shouldered it and made his way back to the southern path.

Hunched against the rain and wind, Sneezle returned to the dryad's pool. The pool was empty. Beneath tree roots he spied a small round door.

Sneezle knocked, then knocked again. Finally the little door opened. The dryad's gaze softened when she saw that Sneezle was trembling.

"Come in from the rain, small one," she said. "Have you brought another story for me?"

"I have, Lady," said Sneezle solemnly, dripping on the floor.

She led him to a plain, dry room below the roots of her elder tree. He sat down gratefully and told her about the little men.

"I've heard this tale before," she said. "An oak tree saw strange little men chasing after some moss maidens. A beech tree saw a pook battered within an inch of his life. A hawthorn said King Oberon sent ten of his finest elfin knights to find these wicked creatures—but then the creatures disappeared."

"The rain makes them dissolve," Sneezle told the dryad. "It turns them into mud."

"Indeed? Then you must go to King Oberon and tell him what you've seen." She cocked her head as though she heard something. All Sneezle heard was wind. "My tree tells me the storm is almost past. Wait here until it's done. I'll make you elderflower tea. You've a long journey ahead."

She served the tea in small wood cups, along with bread of pale green flour. And then she sent him on his way as the sun broke through the clouds.

Following the old dryad's advice, he waded through cold stream water and found a path on the other side leading up to the faery court. But just a little way upstream he stopped, hearing a voice ahead and smelling an unfamiliar salty smell that made him wary. The pathway turned and disappeared from view beyond thick ferns and brush. He tiptoed forward, pushed fern fronds aside. And saw a giant.

It was a giant girl with dark blond hair wearing a long white dress. She held one of the little men in her lap, and she was crying. Beside her was a large black cat, and scattered on the ground below were five more little stick men, lying lifeless on the moss.

"It's hopeless," sobbed the human girl. "I'm just no good at *all*, Dinah. Every faery I make is even uglier than the last one!"

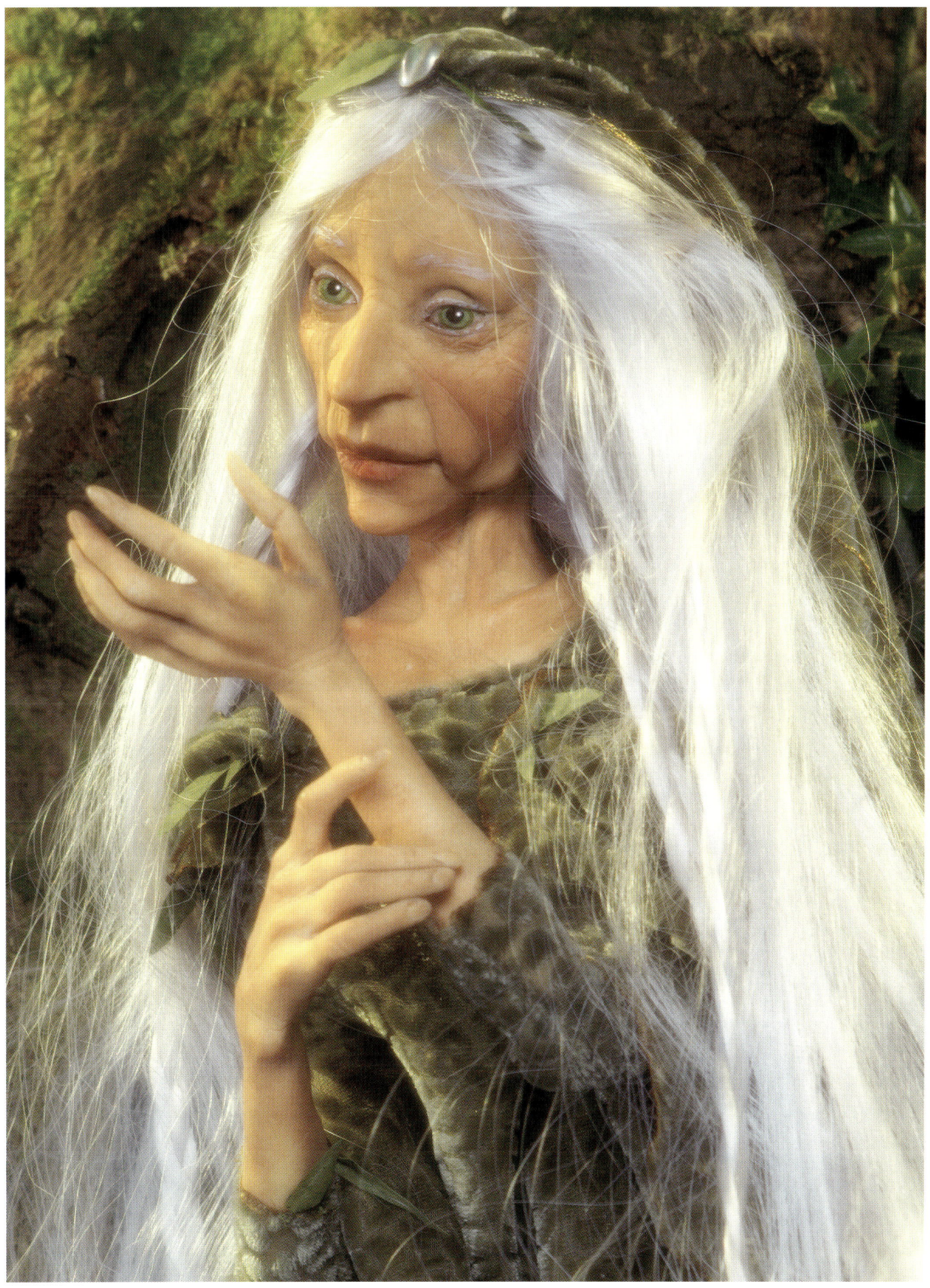

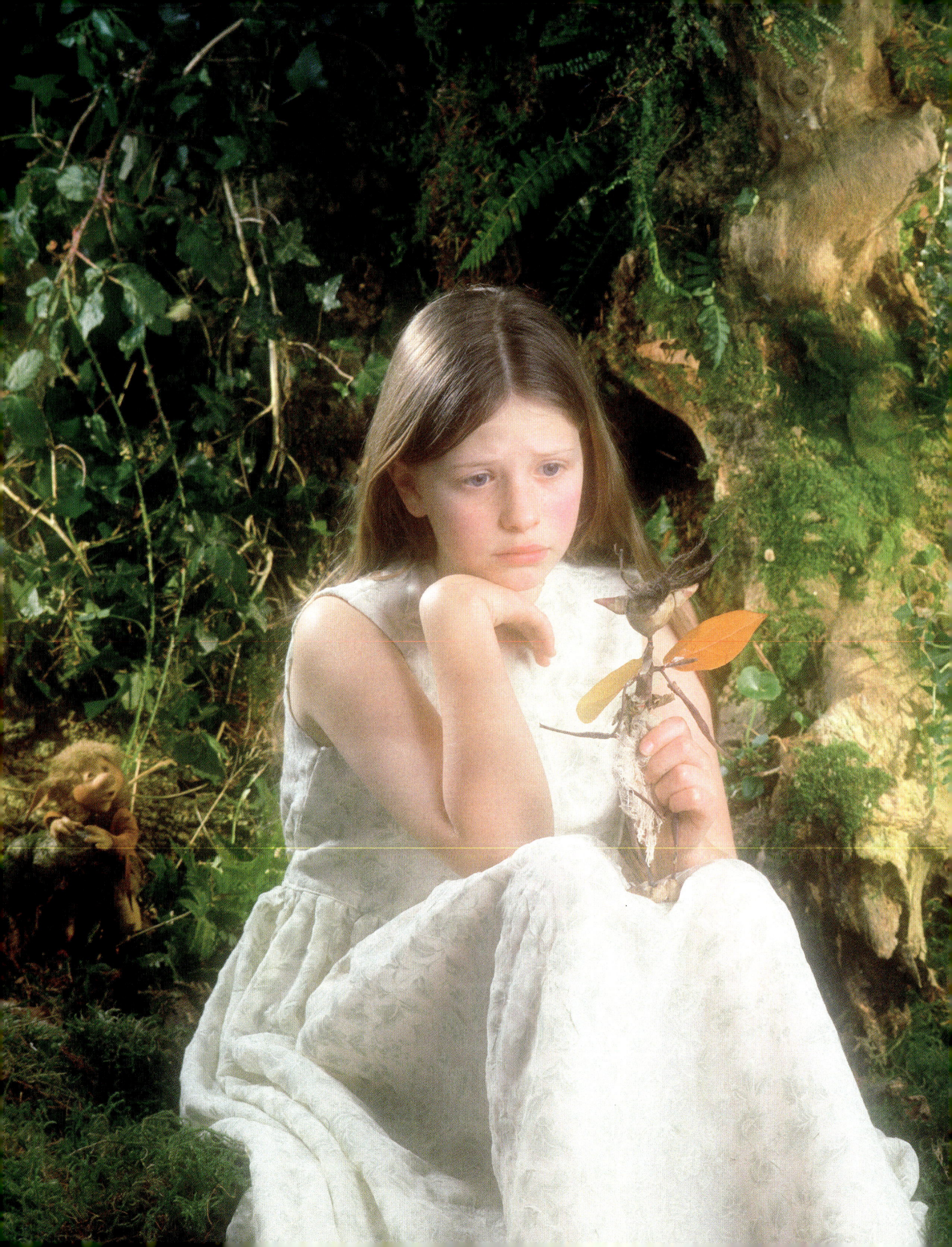

The black cat simply sat and purred, contented with her patch of sun, while giant tears rolled down the big girl's cheeks, falling to her lap.

She wiped her eyes with a grubby hand, then pinched mud from the rain-soaked ground to form a long, sharp nose that she attached to the stick man's face. This one *was* even uglier than the others—his hair made out of weeds, his clothes of leaves stitched clumsily together and scraps of cloth.

Somewhere beyond the trees a voice called, "Rowan!" and the girl looked up, while overhead the rowan trees shivered with pleasure to hear their name.

The big girl stood. "Come on, Dinah. Mum doesn't like us in the woods. We'll leave these poor fellows behind." She put the little man aside and started down the southern path that led out of the forest.

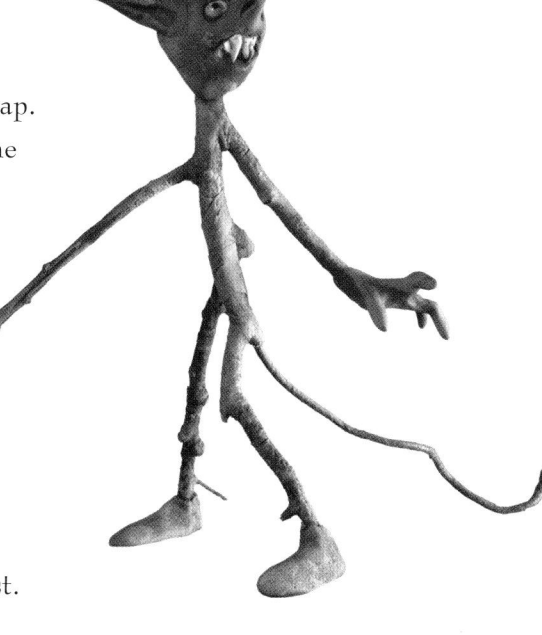

When Sneezle was sure the girl was gone, he crept out of the underbrush . . . and then he turned around and dashed right back to his hiding place. The stick men had begun to move! Their mud heads lolled from side to side, their fingers twitched, and shudders ran through each of the twiggy bodies. Sticks turned into flesh, pebbles into eyes, leaves into clothes and shoes. They lumbered to their feet, snarling and lashing long bristled tails.

Each little man took up a stout oak stick, which turned into a sword, and one grabbed up a mushroom cap, which turned into a shield. With lowing, moaning, snuffling sounds, the hideous creatures banded together and headed straight for Sneezle where he cowered among the ferns.

The boy jumped up, let go of his heavy sword, and ran as fast as he could, leaping over roots and stones as he desperately sought shelter. Ahead, he spied a shadow in the grass and so he dove for it, expecting to tumble down a rabbit hole or brownie den. Instead, he found himself in muffled darkness, cloth beneath his palms. He heard the little men go rushing past, growling and slavering, and he waited motionless until the sound faded in the distance.

Then he heard another sound. The human girl was coming back. He smelled her salty smell and heard her crash through the underbrush.

"Dinah, do you see my book bag anywhere? I left it in the grass—I'm sure I did," Sneezle heard her say. "Oh, there it is!"

The ground beneath him tilted suddenly and swung beneath his feet. He was in the human's bag, tumbling to the bottom as she picked it up. *Oh no!* he thought. He had to get out! But this proved to be impossible. Each time he climbed the slippery cloth to the top, he was knocked back down again. Bruised and trembling with fright, he huddled miserably in the dark. He'd have to wait until she put it down to make his escape.

But where could she be taking him? *Home*, he realized, heart sinking. And that meant he was leaving the woods and heading for the human world.

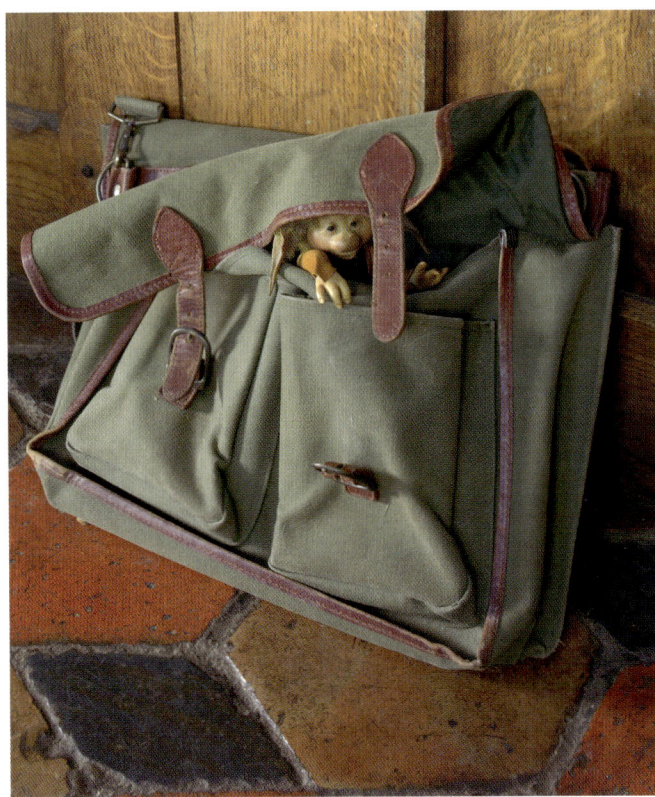

They seemed to travel on forever, the big girl whistling cheerfully while the root faery cowered in the dark; then he felt her footsteps slowing. He heard the creak of an open door. He smelled the scent of bread baking. The girl called, "Mum, I'm home!" and the bag was dropped onto the floor.

Once the bag was motionless, Sneezle made his way slowly to the top and peered out at a giant room full of giant furniture. He poked his head out farther. The big black cat was peering back at him. She bared her teeth and growled at the forest faery, her whiskers twitching.

"Dinah, be quiet!" said Rowan crossly.

The cat made a sudden lunge for Sneezle. He leapt to the floor, cat at his heels until Rowan grabbed Dinah's collar.

"What are you doing, you silly thing? Chasing invisible faeries again?" She picked up the disgruntled cat, who strained to get back down.

Sneezle gaped up at the girl above. The human clearly couldn't see him! But the cat could see him all too well, and he searched for a hiding place.

An older woman, her hair the color of Rowan's, stood across the room. "That cat's not chasing faeries, she's chasing mice," she said, hands on her hips. "Have you been 'feeding the faeries' again? No more crumbs on the hearth, Rowan! You're only attracting mice and bugs and I'm sure we're infested now."

"But, Mum, Grandma says—"

"I don't want to hear what your grandmother says!" her mother interrupted. "Good grief, you're almost ten years old! That's too old to believe in faeries."

"But Grandma—"

"—told you to look after them, I know. But faeries aren't real, Rowan. Your grandmother likes to pretend, that's all. And now that she's sick in the hospital, I need you to help me out around here. It's time to stop playing Make Believe games at your age. Do you understand?"

"Yes, Mum," said Rowan unhappily. She sighed as she put Dinah down.

"Mice," muttered Rowan's mother as Dinah sprang toward Sneezle again.

The little faery turned and ran, scrambled up a cabinet, and wedged himself through the narrow opening of the cabinet's door. He bolted into the dark beyond, and hands grabbed at his arm.

"Is it gone?" said a voice. "Has the Evil Beast been vanquished and destroyed at last?"

"The cat?" asked Sneezle, startled. "No! She's waiting on the floor below!"

"Excellent!" said the voice. "The creature is trapped in the Outer Lands!"

To Sneezle it seemed that they were the ones now trapped, and not the cat outside, but before the boy could make this observation, the voice continued.

"We've thwarted the wicked brute once again! Bravo, bravo to us, gentlemen."

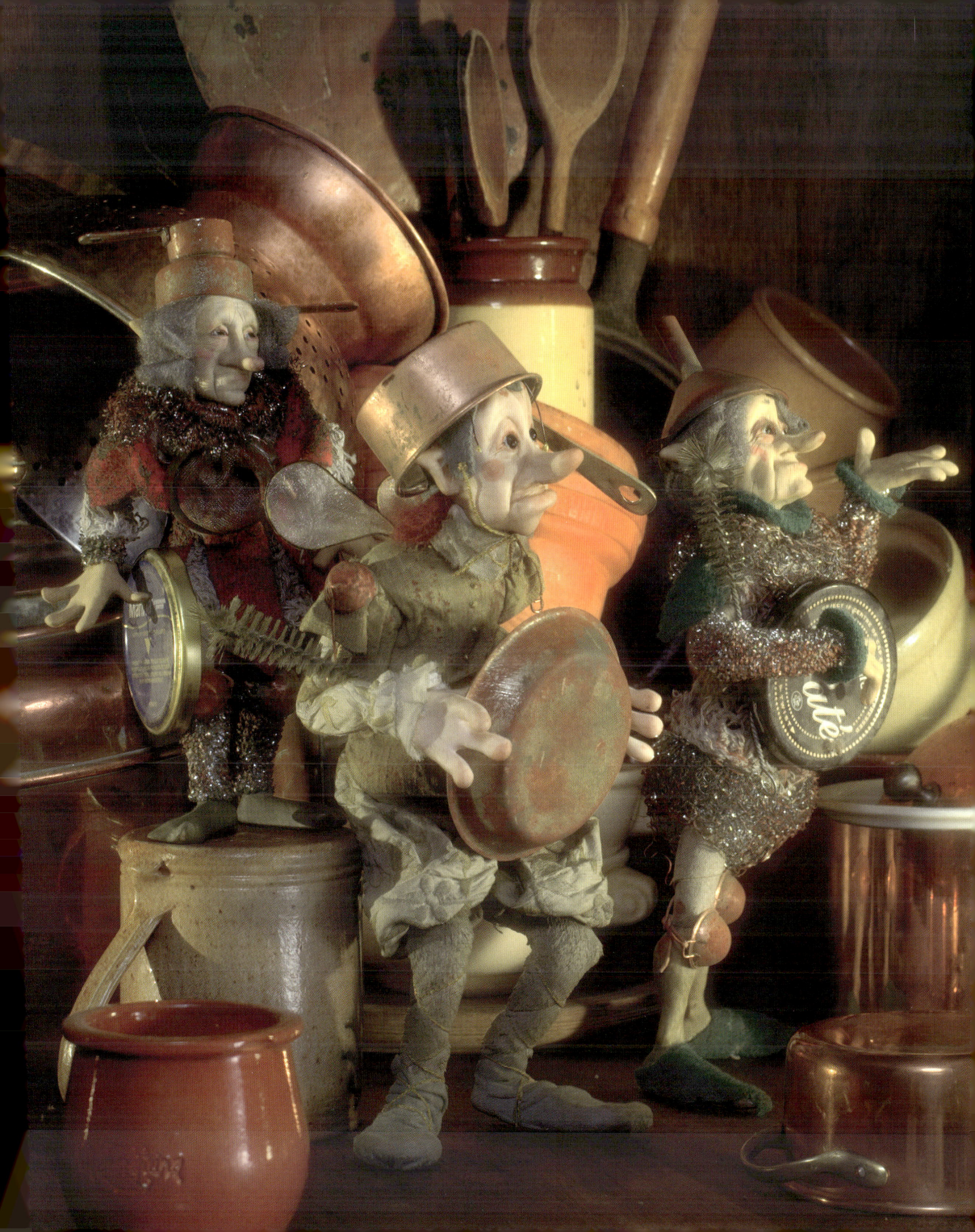

"Capital, capital," said another voice.

"Good show," said a third. "Good show, indeed."

A golden faery light flicked on, illuminating a dusty space that was crammed untidily with enormous cups, saucers, and platters. Three elfin knights looked down at him—the strangest knights he'd ever seen, dressed in silver chain mail and armor made of pots and pans. They carried bottle brushes instead of swords, and shields made out of lids. The knights were old and creaky and the creakiest was the leader.

The lead knight cracked the door open to peer at Dinah, pacing below. "Excellent," he said nervously, backing up. "See how she trembles!"

"She knows that she's no match for us," the second elfin knight agreed.

"What a glorious day this is for faery kind!" the third said pompously. "And a glorious day for you, stranger. Rescued from the jaws of certain death by the greatest warriors in the realm!"

"Excuse me, but what realm *is* this?" Sneezle asked the trio of knights, perplexed.

"The faery realm, you young savage! Ruled by the faery king!" one snapped.

The leader of the band seized Sneezle by the arm again. "But you are not to be blamed for your ignorance. No, boy, you are to be pitied. Prepare yourself to be much amazed, for the court lies just ahead."

He led Sneezle past baking tins, across a series of dusty shelves, and through a hole into a great cavern below the kitchen sink. Here, thick cobwebs swung over their heads among old copper pipes, from which a slow and steady drip leaked water to a tub below.

An old, old faery sat inside the tub. He wore a golden crown—and nothing else, his bony frame half hidden by foaming soap. The room was crowded with courtiers and councilors and serving gnomes, surrounding the king's bathtub and ignoring His Majesty's nakedness.

Sneezle found that he was indeed amazed—not by the court's splendor, but by the oddity of these faeries in manners, looks, and dress. Each one of them was strangely misshapen: too thin, too squat, too long, with cheeks unnaturally white beneath bright circles of red paint. The three knights used their bottle brushes to prod Sneezle ahead of them, pushing the forest faery down to his knees before the tub.

"You may rise," said the king in a reedy voice. "Come closer. Let me see your face. Someone hand me my spectacles." A serving gnome quickly complied, and the naked king put on a pair of enormous broken glasses. "Deary me, what kind of a creature is this? Brownie? Bwbachod? Boggart?"

"I'm a tree root faery, sir, of the hawthorn clan," Sneezle said politely.

"Never heard of such a preposterous thing. Where are you from?" the king demanded.

"From Old Oak Wood," Sneezle explained, "the oldest kingdom in Faerieland, ruled by King Oberon and Queen Titania and . . ." He stopped abruptly, realizing the entire room had fallen into shocked silence.

"What rot is this?" said a high, shrill voice.

He turned and saw a remarkable sight, for the faery queen of the cabinet realm had now entered the room. Her Majesty wore a mildewed dress that seemed to be made of scrubbing

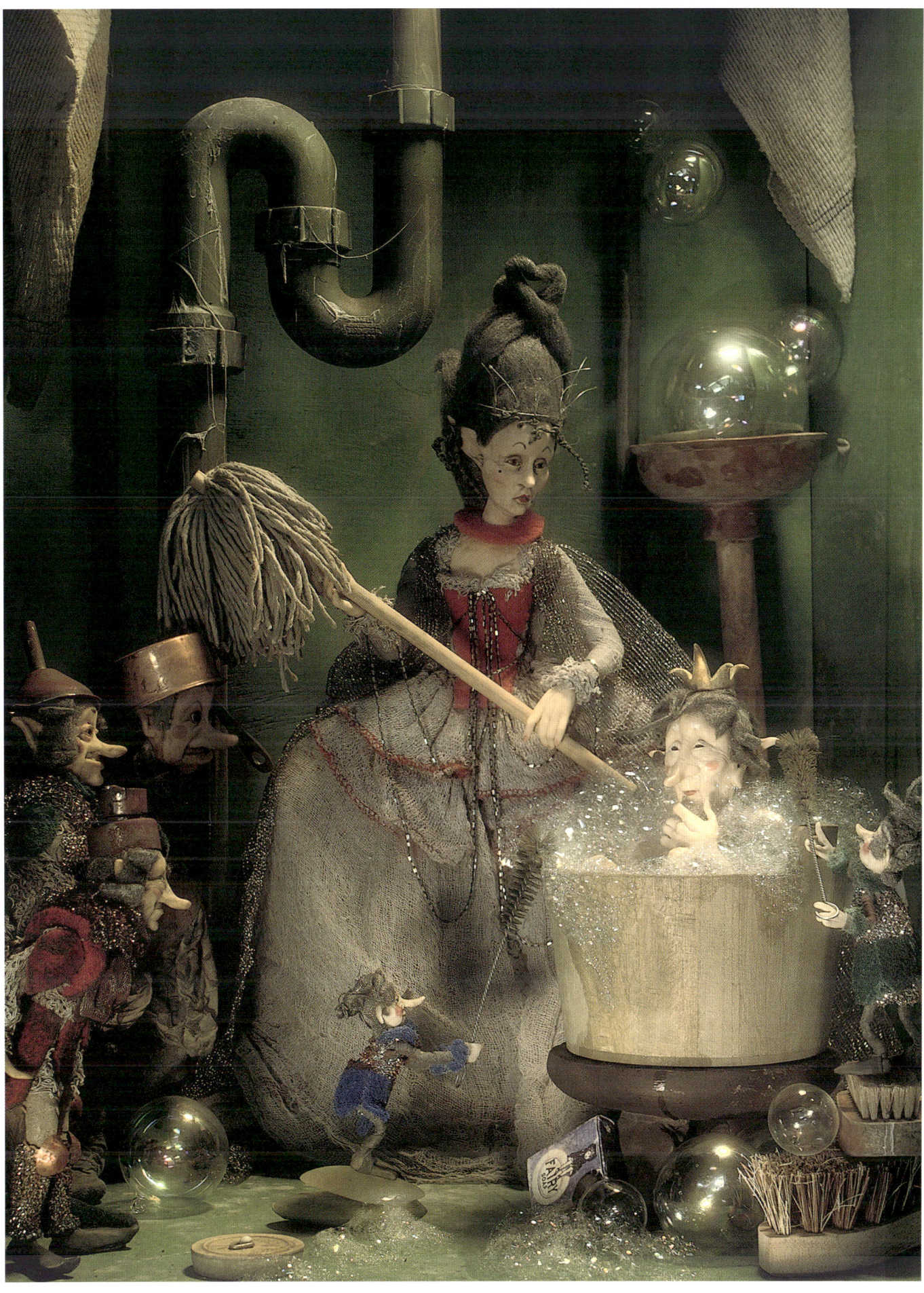

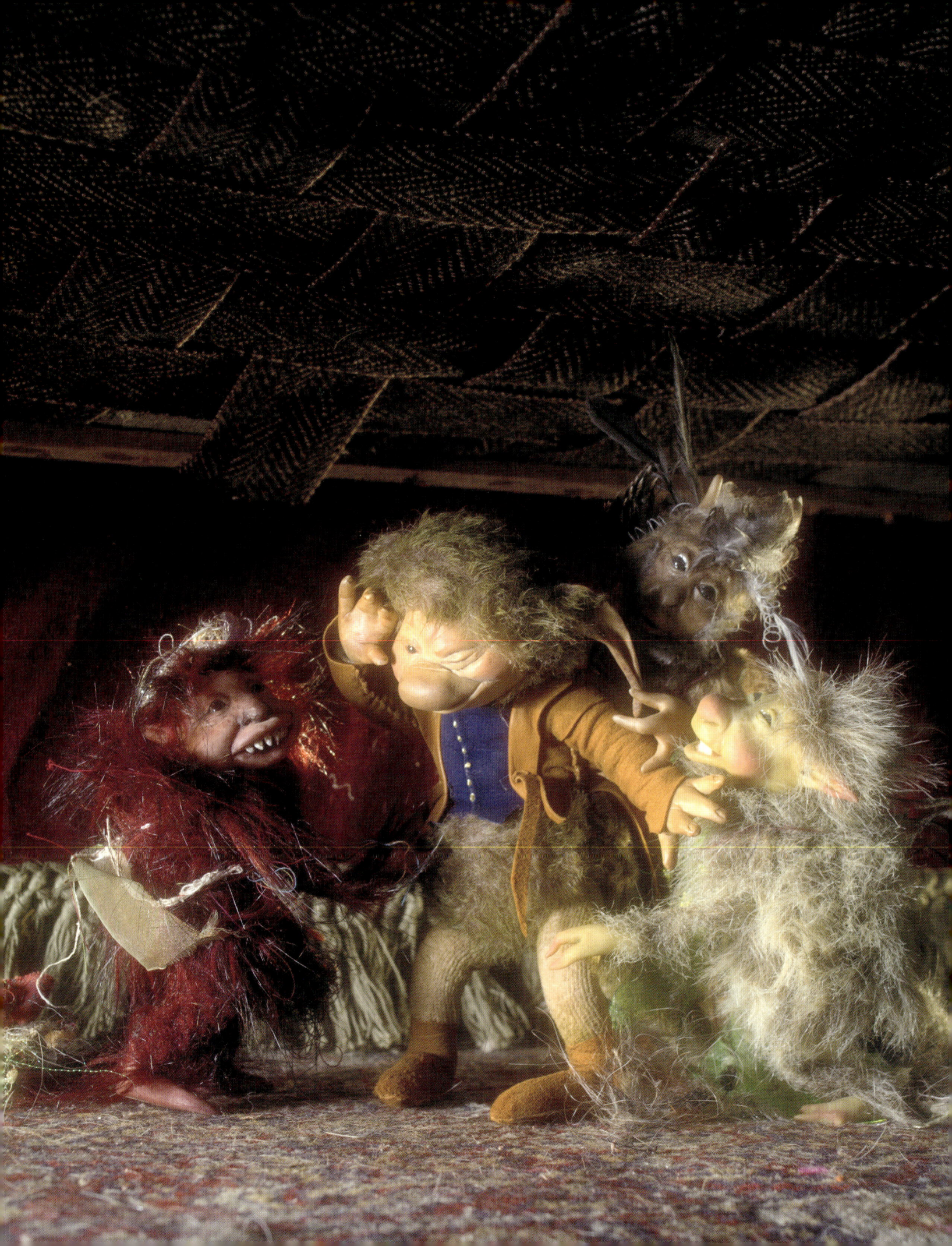

cloths, its long train held by ragged maidens with tattered, useless wings. Her hair was piled up so high that it brushed cobwebs from the pipes above, bound by an elaborate crown of silver filigree.

"What rot is this?" repeated the queen in a voice as loud as the king's was thin. "What's this about other courts and queens?" She prodded Sneezle with a mop.

"Old Oak Wood is the faery court that I come from, your Majesty."

"Rot, I say! For I, Glorinda the Glorious, am queen of Faerieland. And there," she pointed at the tub, "is the great King Mustapha the Mad. Who else would dare to claim the crown? This is treason, little man!"

"Now, now, Glorinda," whined the king. "Treason is a little harsh, perhaps. Forgive this creature's ignorance. He's only a savage, my dear."

"A treasonous savage!" Glorinda roared.

The king sank farther into his tub. "Of course. You're right, as always."

The cabinet queen gave a satisfied smile. "This creature is an Outlander. You know what we do with Outlanders."

"Employ them?" the king suggested, blinking. "We're running rather short on knights, dear one."

Glorinda glared.

King Mustapha tried again. "Send him back to the Outer Lands?"

"Oh yes, do!" cried the knight trio.

"Send him back!" the courtiers chanted.

"See that it's done," said Glorinda the Glorious with a bored wave of her hand.

The knights wielded their brushes to force the boy backward to a cabinet door. It opened and he spied Dinah crouched below, licking her lips.

"No, please," cried Sneezle, grabbing hold of a knight. "Please, sir, don't push me out!"

A chain mail ring popped off into Sneezle's hand as the boy was ripped away, shoved out the door, and sent tumbling to the floor below.

He landed between the cat's two paws, sprang up with horror, and ran for his life, sliding across the floor tiles with Dinah in hot pursuit. The boy fled through the kitchen door and into a large parlor beyond. He ran across a thick carpet, around a series of table legs, then dove into the darkness beneath a huge red velvet sofa. The cat's long arm groped after him. Sneezle pushed himself beyond its reach, sputtering as he moved through cobwebs, fur balls, and clouds of dust.

He tucked the ring in a coat pocket while his eyes adjusted to the gloom. And then he saw that there were other eyes around him—perhaps a dozen of them, gleaming in pale faces topped by caps made of feathers and fuzz. These small creatures were faeries of some sort, formed out of lint and fur and dust and dirt, with long fingers and noses smudged with soot.

They giggled as they surrounded the forest faery, patting his head, his cheeks, pinching him on his arms, his legs, his nose, and his furry bottom.

"Stop!" said Sneezle. "Stop, that hurts!" This only made them pinch harder, and he backed away, slapping at the hands that pinched and poked and prodded. Laughing, they pulled him down to the ground, pinching his belly, pinching his toes. He sneezed and coughed and sputtered and struggled back up to his feet.

Gasping for breath, Sneezle fought his way out from underneath the sofa and clambered up a table leg, with Dinah at his heels once more. The forest faery leapt to a chair . . . a stool . . . a crowded tabletop. A teacup crashed noisily to the floor as he darted through crockery.

The sound brought Rowan into the room. "Dinah, what are you up to now?"

The cat ignored her, intent on catching the faery, and Sneezle ran faster.

Another voice cried, "Quick, over here!" It came from a crooked bookshelf above. A brownie was grinning down at Sneezle, his long brown arm extended.

Sneezle grabbed the brownie's hand as Dinah crouched and prepared to leap.

Rowan grabbed Dinah's collar. "Settle down! Or I'll put you out!"

The thwarted cat slunk back down to the floor, ears flattened with disgust, while Sneezle, safe on the shelf above, gave his rescuer a grateful look.

"I owe you my life!" Sneezle said, panting.

"Think nothing of it," the brownie replied.

The fellow was barely taller than Sneezle, with snapping eyes, long floppy ears, and a red cap perched upon his head. In the woods, the faeries who wore red caps were dangerous and best avoided—but this seemed like a friendly faery. And Sneezle needed a friend.

"Perhaps, young sir," the brownie said, "you'll come rest in my humble home? I dare say we'll be safer there. This way now, if you will."

They climbed up brocade draperies and edged their way around the room on a narrow ledge of wainscoting until they reached the opposite wall. In the corner stood a wardrobe, and on top of it stood a miniature house—built in human style but just the right size for a brownie.

Humble? It was magnificent, consisting of many spacious rooms, each of them richly furnished and hung with sumptuous tapestries. "This house was made for dolls," the brownie explained. "Rowan used to play with it, but then she put her dolls away and forgot them. So I moved in." He led Sneezle through a front parlor, a library, a snooker room, and then into a fine conservatory, lit by tall candles. "Make yourself comfortable, good sir. And let me introduce myself. I'm Billy Blind, of the house brownie tribe, entirely at your service."

"I'm Sneezle," said the boy. "I come from Greenmoss Glen in Old Oak Wood."

"You're from the woods? Then you must be on a mission! A quest!" Billy's eyes grew bright.

"I *was* on a mission," Sneezle admitted, "but now I'm just plain lost, Billy."

The brownie patted the downcast faery's shoulder. "I'll fetch refreshments, sir. Nothing looks quite so bad on a full stomach."

Sneezle agreed.

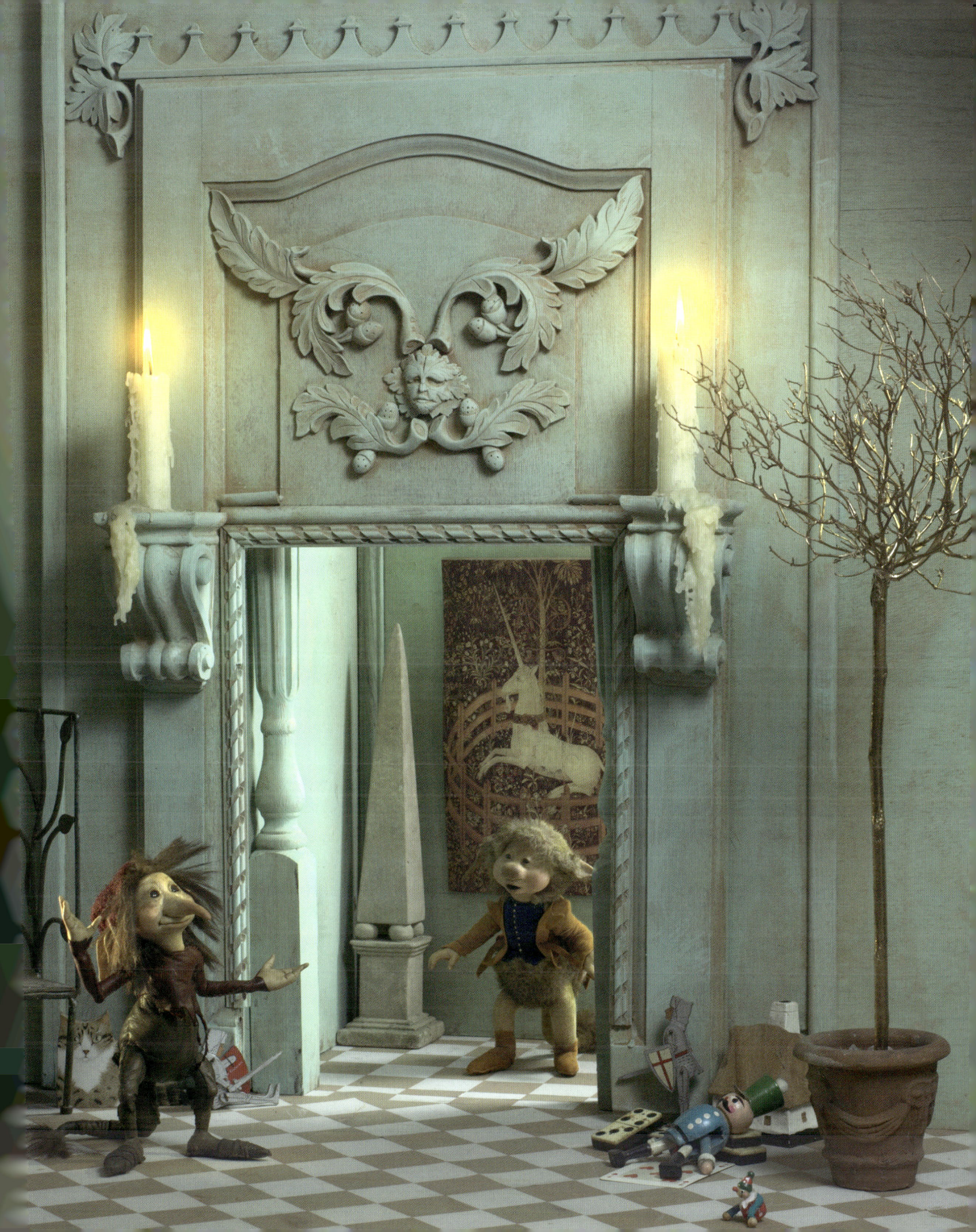

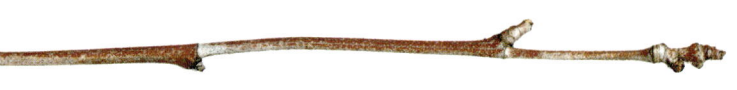

The brownie left the room and soon returned carrying a silver tray laden with sticky buns, pink cakes, and mugs of gooseberry cider. Sneezle applied himself to eating, and when his belly was finally full he pushed his plate aside and told the house brownie his story.

"All I want to do is go home," the boy concluded miserably. "But how will I ever get past Dinah? And all those horrid stick men?"

"Alas, if only my mistress were here," the brownie said regretfully. "She'd help you."

"Who's your mistress, and where has she gone?" Sneezle asked his host.

The brownie sighed. "My dear mistress was the wisest woman on the moor. She lived here all her life until she took ill during the last full moon—and then they took her away to the place where the Big Peoples' healers live."

Sneezle looked at the other, astonished. "Your mistress is a human being?"

"Of course," said Billy. "I keep her house tidy. That's what we house brownies do, young sir. We serve our mistress, and she serves us. She leaves us cookies and milk and toast, and sings to us, and gives us presents. It's reciprocal, I assure you."

"But faeries serving the Big People?" The very thought made Sneezle shudder.

"Big People are just like us—there's good and there's bad," said Billy Blind. "Though lately, of course, it's harder to find a house where an honest house brownie can live. These modern, newfangled humans don't believe in us," he sniffed.

"Is that why Rowan couldn't see me?"

"Most humans can't," the brownie explained. "Only a few see faeries now. Special ones, like my mistress. She's an artist," Billy added proudly.

"What's an 'artist'?" Sneezle asked him, puzzled by the unfamiliar word.

"A sorcerer," his host said promptly. "Art is one way that humans make magic." The house brownie grew solemn then, his long brown ears and tail sagging. "But ever since my mistress left, I fear her magic has been unraveling. A faery-infested house, you see, can be a tricksy kind of thing. Not all house faeries are helpful ones. Some are wild, some are wicked, some are wily creatures indeed. And even the best can turn feral without a good master or mistress to mind them."

Sneezle patted the bruises on his arm. "Do feral faeries pinch?"

"They do indeed. Our mistress knew how to keep those wild boys in line. But while she's away, her daughter—that's Rowan's mother—neglects them shamefully. And now they've gone out of control." He shook his brown head sadly.

"But why does she neglect them?" asked Sneezle.

"She doesn't believe in faeries anymore. She did once upon a time, when she was a child . . . but not as a woman grown. She's forgotten us. And the wild boys grow wilder every day."

"But what about the girl?" asked Sneezle.

"Young Rowan?" The brownie gave a sigh. "The girl is caught between two worlds—the old ways of her grandmother and her mother's newfangled ideas. She longs to see us faeries, but can't. She *almost* believes in us, but not quite. I pray the mistress can teach her to see us one day, if she ever returns."

"But what if your mistress doesn't return?" pressed Sneezle, for the house brownie looked troubled.

"Well then," the other replied gravely, "I hope you'll be back in your woods, young sir. The wild ones here will grow worse still, and one day I'll turn feral myself. That's what happens to neglected house brownies, you see. We turn into boggarts."

Boggarts. Sneezle knew the word. He'd never encountered them in the woods, but every faery child had heard of boggarts, who were worse than goblins.

The boy looked deeply into the kindly eyes of the house brownie beside him. It was hard to imagine this courteous creature turning into a hideous boggart.

"Is that what happened," Sneezle asked, "to those mean little dust devils under the couch? Are they boggarts now?"

"That's exactly what happened! They used to be cheerful little creatures who kept the cottage corners swept, but they're boggarts now. Stay away from them, boy. You're lucky you only got pinched!"

Sneezle's spirits sank lower. Boggarts. Cats. Stick men. And Big People. How would he ever get past them all and back to his own dear forest? He said, "I may not ever get home—but if I find a way, Billy, then you should come along with me. It's dangerous in this cottage!"

Billy smiled but shook his head. "Spring Cottage is my home, Sneezle. I'd pine if I ever left this place, just as you pine for your hawthorn trees. I only wish I knew how to help you get back to your forest." The house brownie paused suddenly and put a finger to his chin. "It occurs to me that there is another faery here who might help you. Her name is Aurora. I haven't met her, but the mistress thinks highly of her."

"Where can I find her?" Sneezle asked.

"In my mistress's workshop, down the hall."

Sneezle swallowed. How would he ever get there, with Dinah waiting?

Billy, however, had a plan. "You could travel through the mouse corridors. They have their own dangers, it's true, but you'd be safe from Dinah there. Spring Cottage, you see, is riddled with passageways within the floors and walls. The mice in these passages are as meek as . . . well, mice. They won't do you any harm. But you must beware of the rat faeries, who are rather unpleasant creatures."

"I'm not afraid," the forest faery lied in a small, unconvincing voice. The rat faeries of Old Oak Wood were fierce and unpredictable.

"Perhaps I should go along with you? We'll stick to the shadows and the rats will never know."

Sneezle was touched by the brownie's offer, yet he squared his shoulders and said stoutly, "I must go alone, Billy, for one can hide better than two."

"I'm afraid you're probably right," Billy conceded. "But take my sword, young sir. I really must insist upon it. Its name is Courage, and courage is what you'll need should trouble arise. It was my uncle's uncle's sword, and it will serve you well."

"I mustn't take your ancestral sword, Billy! What if I don't return?"

"Then some day your nephew's nephew will carry it proudly," said the generous brownie.

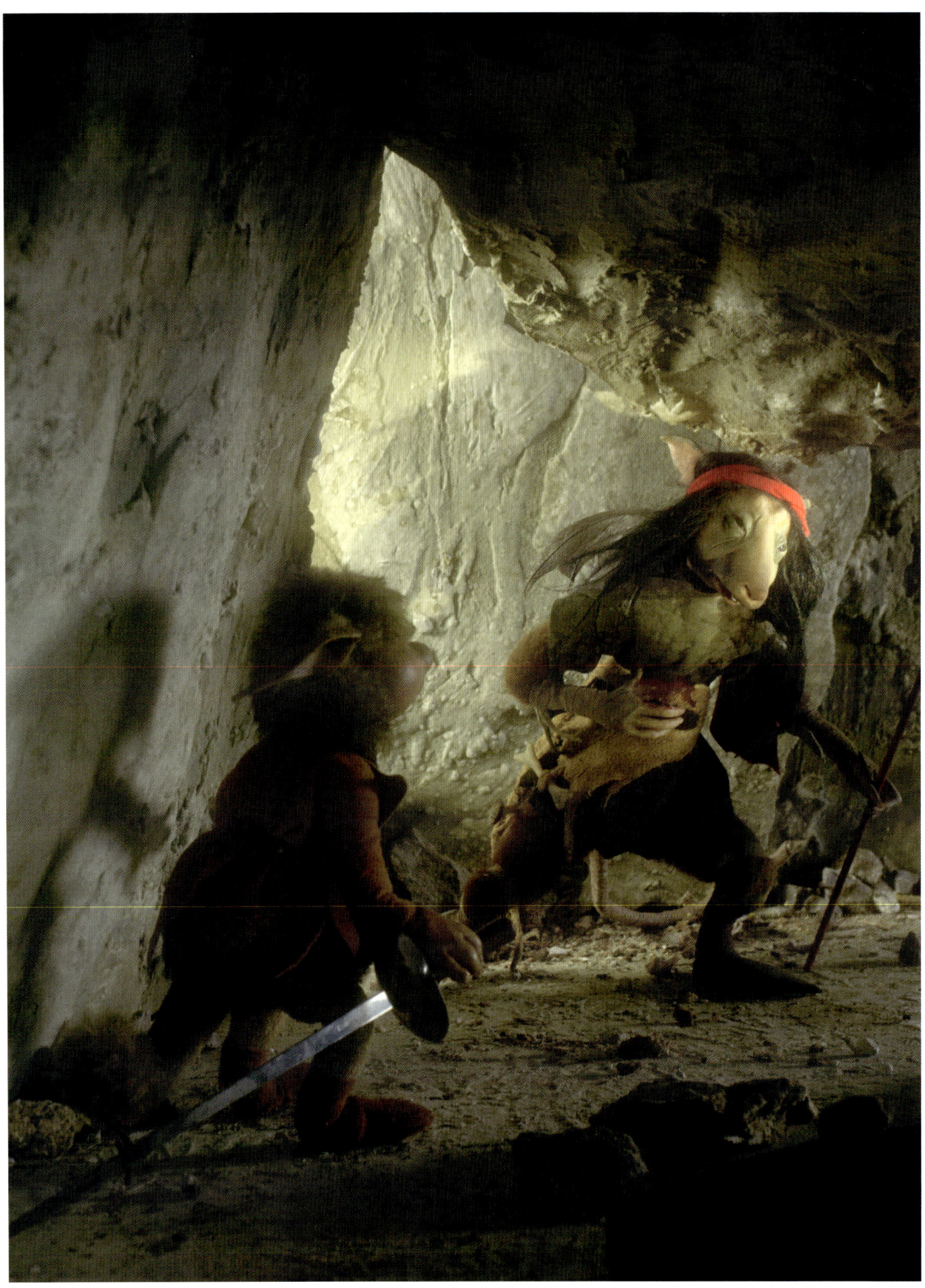

The mouse corridors were a maze of passageways that ran through thick cob walls, underneath the dusty floorboards, and beneath the thatched roof of the cottage. Sneezle entered the corridors through a mouse hole at the wardrobe's foot, while Dinah paced nearby, scenting the faery but unable to reach him.

Inside the walls, the air was dark and gloomy, and he crept forward slowly, holding Courage in two hands, reciting Billy's directions. *Turn right. Turn left.* He sank back into the shadows each time he heard footsteps—families of mice, and a dust faery in the company of a big black beetle. *Turn left. Turn right. Turn right again.* The passage slanted sharply down. The musty air smelled damper now, and something moved ahead.

A shadowed shape came toward him. It had round ears. Ah, just another mouse. Sneezle relaxed his grip on Courage and stepped forward with a friendly smile. The dark figure stepped forward, too, moving into a slat of light. And Sneezle's knees turned to water, for it was a rat faery.

The faery stood taller than Sneezle, a fighting stick gripped in his hand, his eyes gleaming with malice beneath a tangle of long black hair. He wore a jerkin of patched leather with charm-stones knotted to his belt. Around his brow was tied the blood-red cloth of high warrior rank.

"Who goes there?" demanded the rat faery.

"S-s-sneezlewort Boggs," the boy stuttered.

"And where are you going, S-s-sneezlewort Boggs?" the rat faery mocked him, sneering.

"I seek the mistress's workshop," said Sneezle. "Truly, s-s-sir, I mean no harm."

"Then why come armed into our realm? Nay, why come into our realm at all?"

The rat faery stepped closer, pointing his fighting stick at Sneezle.

"Get back to the world above, young Boggs," he hissed, his beady eyes narrowed. His mildewed clothes smelled of damp places. His whiskers twitched menacingly.

The forest faery trembled but held his ground. "I can't go back above. I need to get to that workshop, and there's a cat prowling in the hall."

"A beast above and a beast below. You'll have to choose then, S-s-sneezlewort Boggs. Which of us is more dangerous?" The faery smiled nastily.

"I think you're probably both quite dangerous," said Sneezle in a small voice. "P-p-please, I didn't come here to fight."

"Too bad," said the rat faery.

He raised his stick. Sneezle raised his sword, but the stick knocked Courage from his hands. Then suddenly the rat faery went down, blood staining his jerkin.

Sneezle stood for a moment, confused. Then he knelt beside the rat faery, pushed the bloody jerkin aside, and saw a great wound beneath. "You were hurt before you met me!" he cried.

"Boggarts." The faery spit out the word.

"Boggarts? Down here?"

"Seven of them," the other gasped between clenched teeth. "Trying to get into our realm. They were—"

"No, save your breath," the boy urged. "You're bleeding. We need to find a healer. Take my arm and I'll help you stand."

"But why help *me*?" the warrior demanded.

"Because you're hurt. Put your arm around my shoulder . . ."

"You're not a boggart, then?"

"A boggart? Don't be ridiculous!" said Sneezle indignantly.

With his arm around the boy's shoulders, the warrior found that he could walk, leaning heavily on the smaller faery, his face ashen with effort. Before too long they spied the glow of golden faery light ahead, and then a troop of rat faery soldiers rushed forward to claim their comrade.

"Prince Miko!" cried an elderly soldier. His warrior cloth was midnight blue, and the painted staff he carried seemed more elaborate than the others. "You there," he said, pointing to another soldier. "Go fetch the healers at once. And you two, carry the prince to his bed. Carefully, carefully now!"

The soldiers lifted their wounded prince and laid him down in a nest of furs. A slender soldier knelt on the floor beside him, eyes bright with tears.

"It's only a scratch, my dear," the prince rasped out. "It's nothing. The healers will fix it."

"You fool!" she said, gazing at him fiercely. "You dust-brained mouse! You idiot!"

The elderly faery turned to Sneezle. His hair and his rat whiskers were gray, but he carried himself with all of the grace and power of a warrior still. "Tell us what happened to our prince," he demanded.

"He fought against seven boggarts," said Sneezle.

The female soldier sucked in a sharp breath. "Idiot!" she repeated.

"How is it that you came to his aid—a house faery, and our enemy?" The old faery looked Sneezle up and down, puzzled by him.

"I'm not a house faery," Sneezle explained, "but a tree root faery from Old Oak Wood. And yes, I'm a little frightened of rats, but I'm not an *enemy*."

The slender soldier rose. A crown glimmered behind her warrior band. She took the boy's hands in her own and said, "What do they call you?"

"Sneezle," he mumbled, suddenly shy.

"Then I thank you, Sneezle," the rat princess replied, "for the gift of my fool brother's life. What boon can we give you in return? Gold? Jewels? A fine wheel of cheese?"

"All I want, Princess," said Sneezle, "is to go back home to Old Oak Wood."

She frowned. "Your forest is far outside our realm. I cannot help you, boy."

"Then help me get to the mistress's workshop. There may be someone there who can."

She peered at Sneezle, unsmiling, through tangled black hair much like her brother's. He forced himself to hold her gaze, and her look changed to approval. "Your courage has earned you safe passage through our realm, Sneezle of Old Oak Wood. If ever you have need of us, just whistle thrice and we shall come."

"Do you know how to whistle, S-s-Sneezlewort?" the wounded prince said, grinning.

"Yes, I do, your R-r-royal Highness," Sneezle stuttered deliberately.

"Idiots!" said the princess, rolling her eyes at both of them.

The princess was as good as her word. She sent four of her best warriors to escort the boy through the mouse corridors all the way to the mistress's workshop. They led him to a hole in the wall where Sneezle got down on his knees to peer into a crowded room dimly lit by a full moon's light. The workshop's single door was shut; the room was empty of humans and cats. He took his leave of the rat soldiers and crawled into the room.

Inside, the boy put down his sword, shimmied up a table leg, and found himself in the strangest place that he had ever been. Everywhere that he looked were faeries—short and

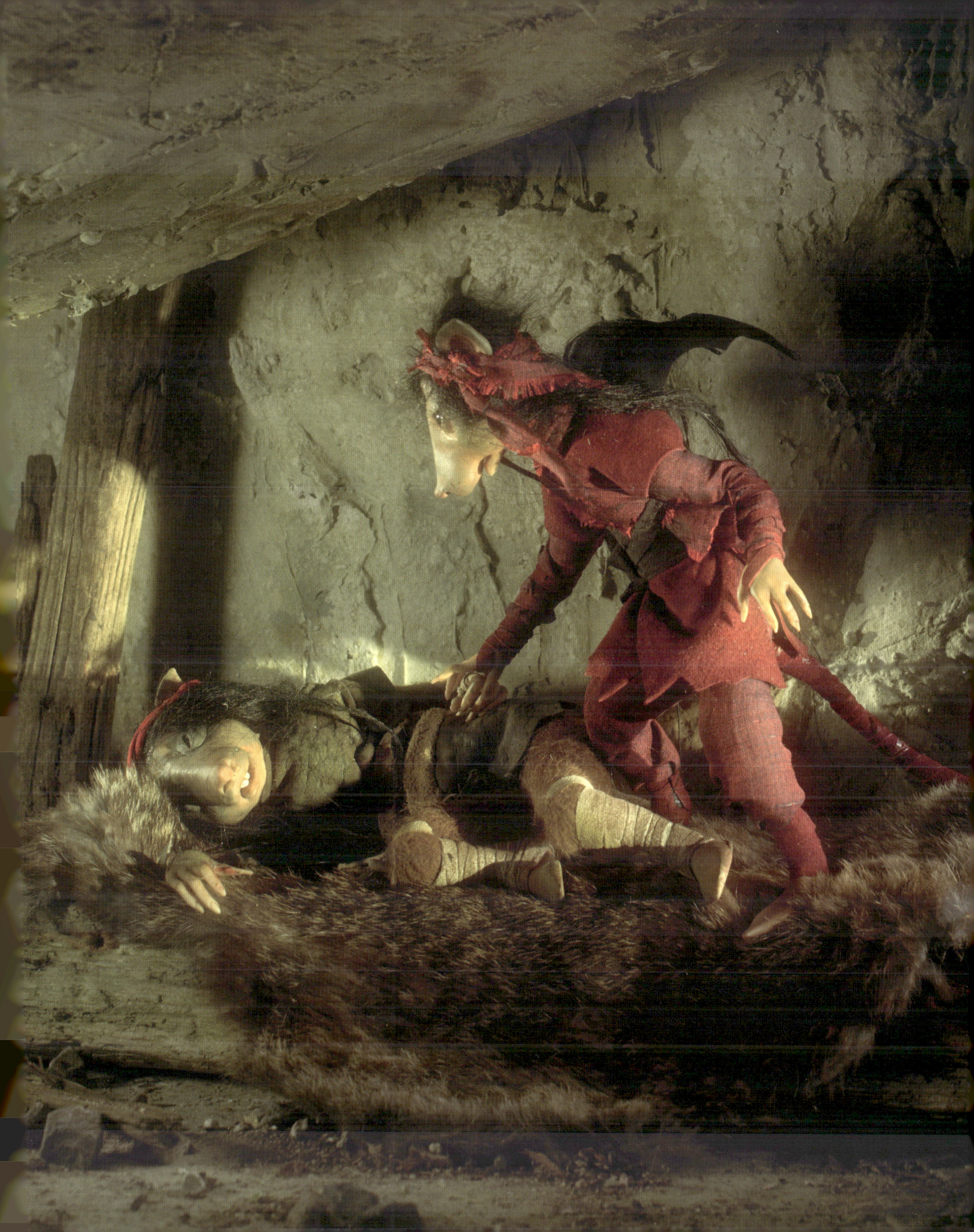

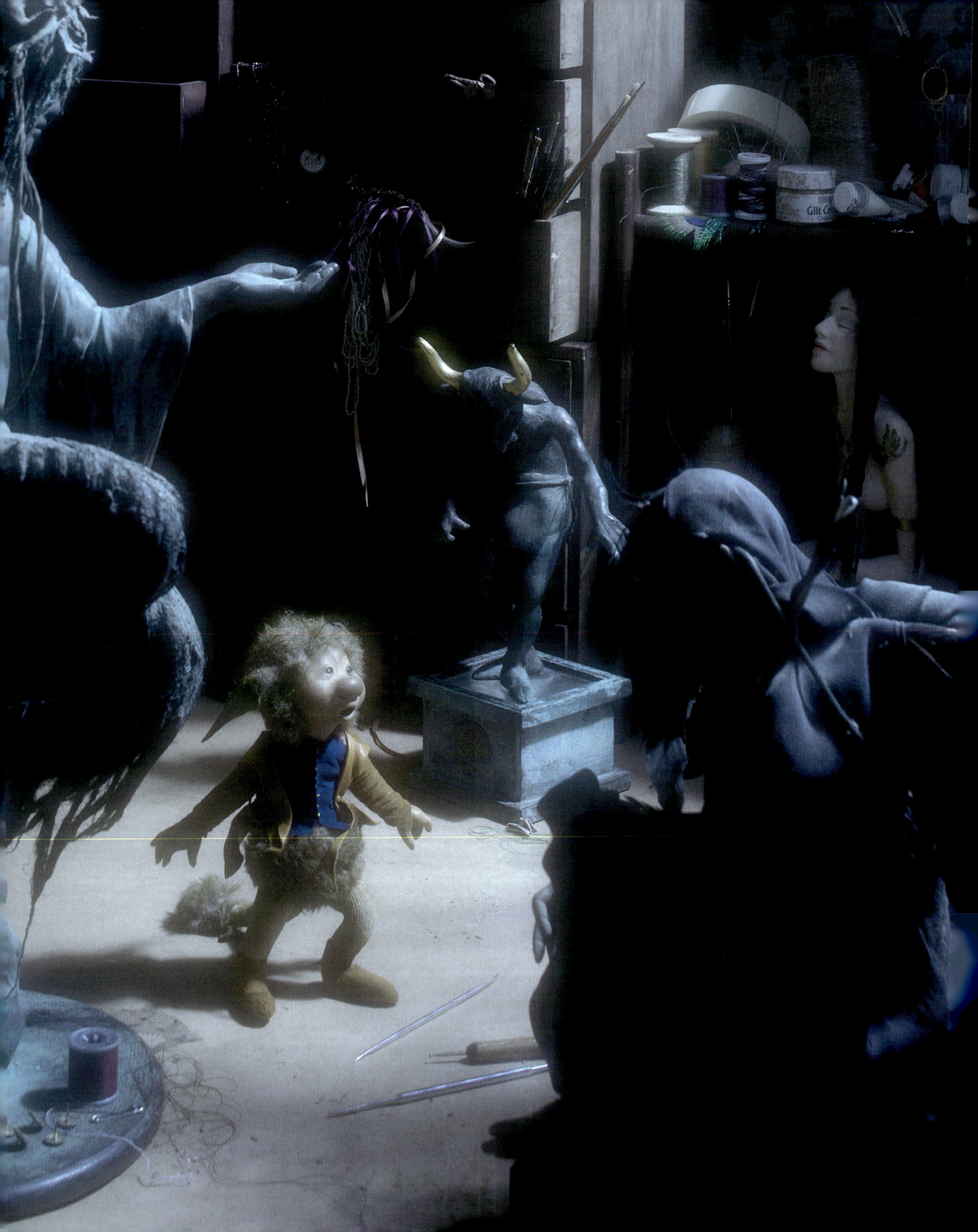

tall, fat and thin, lovely faeries and ugly faeries, and everything in between. But the faeries stood as still as statues, as though frozen by sorcery—frozen in motion, the folds of their clothing lightly covered with dust. He walked among them, wondering what terrible spell could have happened here. Then he brushed against an elf and gasped, for it wasn't real!

They were only dolls. Every one of them—so beautifully made they almost seemed to breathe. *So this*, Sneezle thought in wonder, *is the magic the mistress makes*.

He passed a group of flower maidens, a breathtaking faery with long gold braids, a handsome pair of unicorns, a winged baby sucking her thumb. Somewhere in this eerie room lived the faery that he'd come looking for. Aurora. Sneezle softly called her name, but no one answered.

"Lady Aurora?" he called again. "I'm Sneezle. Billy Blind sent me." He peered at the crowded shelves high above his head. Doll eyes stared back.

He crossed the table, worried now. Perhaps Aurora had gone away. Perhaps there were no real faeries at all, only these dolls. He passed a dark angel, a Minotaur, a sphinx with feathery wings. "Aurora?" he called, his voice cracking. "Please, Lady, are you here?"

But no, it seemed that she wasn't there, for nothing moved and nothing breathed. Dispirited, the faery climbed back down to the workshop's dusty floor . . . and stumbled over something that lay nearby. A tiny hand.

Sneezle bent down and peered more closely. Yes, it *was* a small, white hand—perfectly formed but broken at the end of its slender wrist. The boy looked up to the table above and saw a violet faery there, her arms outstretched. At the end of one graceful arm the hand was missing.

It's only a doll, Sneezle told himself—but she seemed to be looking down at him, her wistful gaze piercing his heart even if she wasn't real. He tucked

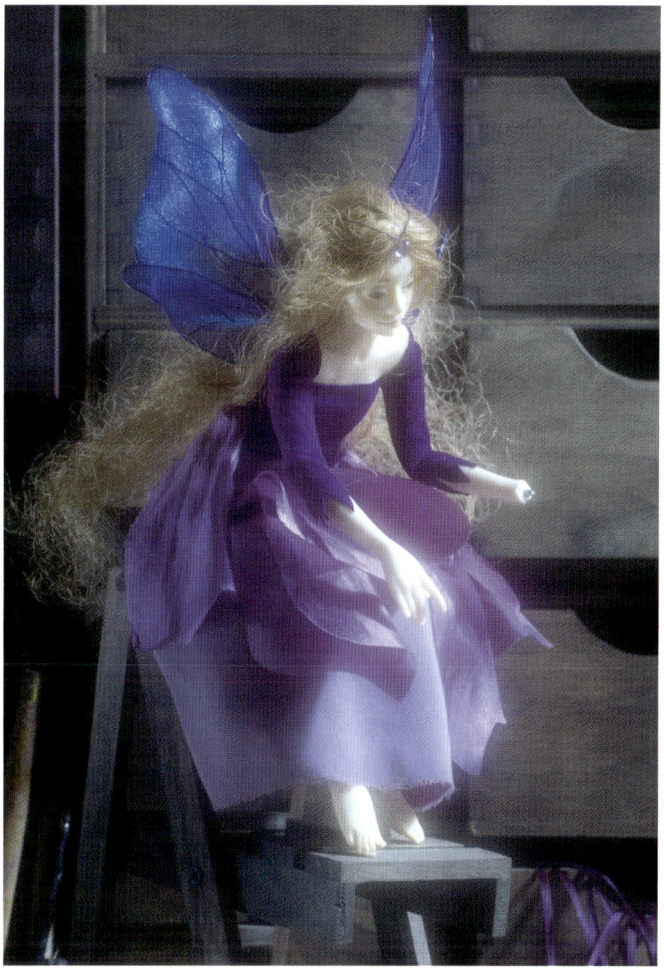

the hand into his pocket, climbed back up to the tabletop, and stood before a flower faery with skirts like violet petals.

Now, how could he put her hand back on? He had no glue, no magic spells. He searched the crowded tabletop, but found nothing there to help him. The little faery rubbed his chin in thought, and then he had an idea. Beneath his gold waistcoat he wore a sash knotted around his waist—his favorite sash, but the sad-eyed doll seemed to need it more than he did. Carefully, he put the small white hand back on the maiden's arm, bound the wrist up with his sash, and knotted it securely. "I hope this helps," he told the doll, "at least until your mistress returns." Then he turned to go, and a sigh rustled through the room like a gentle wind.

"You called my name?" came a voice behind him.

He spun around. The doll had moved! The violet faery was standing now and gazing happily at her hand—but it was another doll who'd spoken, the beautiful woman with golden braids. She walked toward him, her wings lightly fanning the air. Sneezle bowed before her.

The woman laughed. "You needn't bow to me, child. I am not a queen."

"What are you, then?" he asked boldly.

"A faery, like yourself," she said, motioning the boy to come closer. "I'm called Aurora. And also Dawn, and Hope, among other things."

"I called you, Lady, but you didn't answer," said Sneezle. "I thought you were a doll."

"I was," said Aurora, sweeping back her golden hair and smiling at him. "Until your kindness to Violet compelled me to show you my true face."

"Are all of these dolls alive, then?" asked Sneezle, looking around with a nervous gaze.

The lovely woman laughed again. Tiny bells tinkled in her hair. "Of course not, child. The mistress is good, I grant you, but she's not *that* good. It takes rare magic to bring us to life—a meeting of heart, hand, mind, and fate. If this happens but a few times in an artist's life, she's been fortunate."

"The mistress made you?" Sneezle tried to understand.

"No, child, she only made this shape. But the magic of that making summoned me to inhabit it."

The woman stretched luxuriantly, as though she'd just woken from sleep. Other dolls were moving as well: the violet faery, the tawny sphinx, a boy with stag horns on his head. The rest remained empty of life, but these three watched him curiously. Violet smiled and blew Sneezle a kiss, which made him blush.

Aurora sat on a box of sculpting tools, arranging her skirts around her. "What purpose brings you, little man?" she asked the young faery kindly.

"I come from Old Oak Wood," Sneezle explained. "I'm trying to get home."

"I see. It's most unusual to find a forest faery here. A tree root faery, no less. How is it you came to Spring Cottage, child?"

Sneezle began his story at the beginning, telling of the old dryad, the little men, the rainstorm, and hiding in Rowan's book bag.

"You say that Rowan made dolls," said Aurora eagerly, "and they came to life?"

"Yes, but ugly dolls! They came to life after she left."

"Perhaps it's the magic of the woods that woke her dolls so easily. Still," Aurora added, pleased, "the girl must have strong magic, too, or else she couldn't have made the creatures, faery forest or not."

"If she's got magic, it's *bad* magic," Sneezle protested. "Those little men were *mean*!"

"It's not the magic that's bad, child. I'm certain that Rowan meant no harm. You see, a doll can come to life only if a faery inhabits its form. When I was summoned to this shape, the mistress was filled with pride and pleasure in the doll she'd made. But you tell me that you saw Rowan crying as she made her dolls. She's a very lonely child, you know. And angry at her grandmother's loss. The faeries that come to such a calling aren't likely to be nice ones."

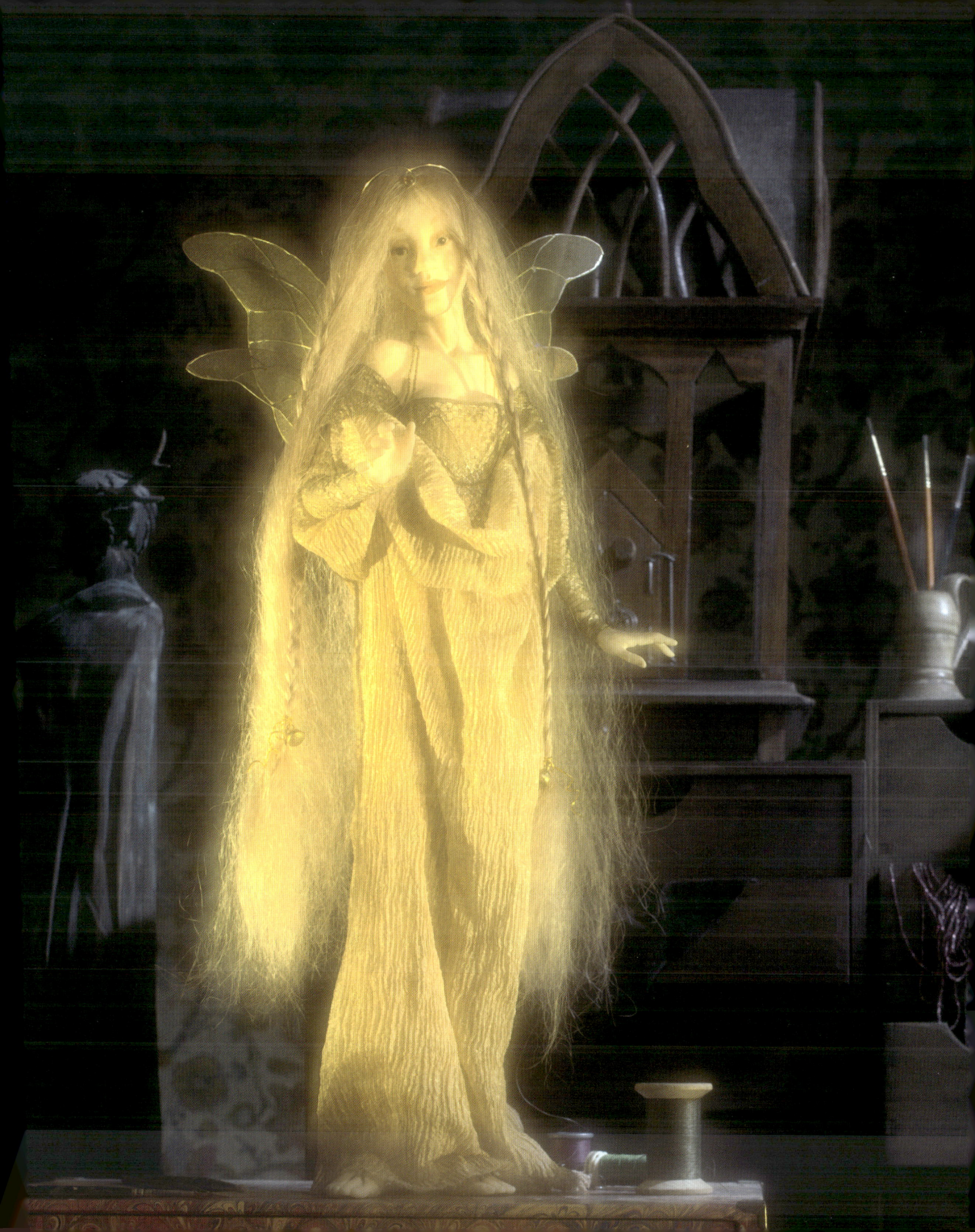

"Those little men were angry, all right."

Aurora gazed at him thoughtfully. "Sometimes, Sneezle, anger is just the other side of fear."

"I don't care! Just make her stop! They're hurting the woodland folk!" he cried.

"How can I make her stop, child, when Rowan can neither hear me nor see me?"

Sneezle knelt before her on one knee. "Please, can you help me get home? I must tell our king about these men so he knows what he is fighting."

The faery shook her head sadly. "As long as I inhabit this form, I'm as bound to this place as any house faery. I don't even leave this workshop—how could I get you back to your forest?"

Sneezle heaved an enormous sigh that seemed to rise from the depths of his soul. "But I *have* to get back," he whispered. Every hour away from the hawthorn trees made his heart hang heavier. He blinked back sudden tears.

The golden woman leaned forward to stroke the forest faery's brow. "Don't give up hope, little man. There's someone else you must talk to. A faery who is wiser than I. Perhaps he'll be able to help you."

"Lady, now where must I go?"

"To see the Old One," she advised.

"And where is he?"

"At the very top of the grandfather clock standing in the hall." Aurora untied a bell from her golden braids and placed it in his palm. "Take this, little man. It's magic, of course. Use it when you need it most. Now go, and quickly, Sneezle, for the hour is growing late."

Go? But he had questions still. "First, can you tell me—" he began.

But the woman before him was only a doll, one finger held up to her lips. The other dolls had frozen, too, posed differently than they'd been before. Violet still blew a kiss, but she was immovable now.

Sneezle made another low bow to Aurora and whispered, "Thank you, Lady." Then he pocketed her bell and climbed down from the tabletop. Taking hold of Courage, he crawled back to the hidden corridors. To his surprise, the rat soldiers were still there waiting for him.

"Where to next?" said a rat faery with a big black patch over one eye.

"To the grandfather clock."

"Righty-o," said the soldier, giving Sneezle a smart salute.

They reached the clock without mishap, and the soldiers lifted him up to it, standing one upon another to boost Sneezle high enough. A chain dangled down the clock's center and a long brass arm swung back and forth. The boy grabbed hold of the chain and climbed, ducking each time the arm passed by, hauling himself up and up with effort, and finally reached the top.

He squeezed himself past levers and gears and found himself in an upper room where large brass wheels turned in a steady rhythm, clicking and clacking. In the very center of the room, lit by the light of a fat candle, was a high wood stool—upon which sat a house brownie, fast asleep. The Old One was very old indeed, with wisps of hair turned white as snow beneath the brown peaked cap that marked him as a sorcerer.

"Sir?" said Sneezle.

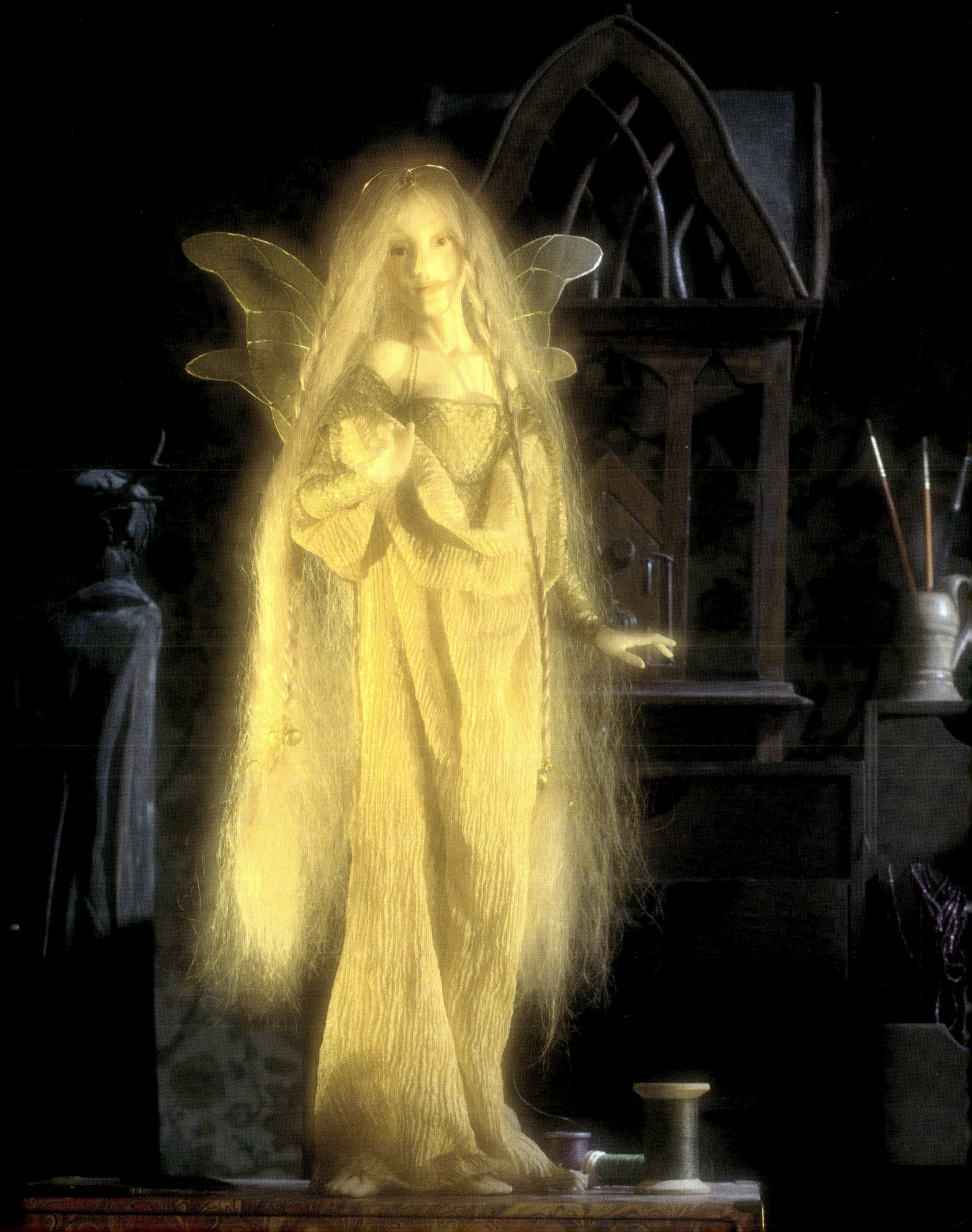

"Those little men were angry, all right."

Aurora gazed at him thoughtfully. "Sometimes, Sneezle, anger is just the other side of fear."

"I don't care! Just make her stop! They're hurting the woodland folk!" he cried.

"How can I make her stop, child, when Rowan can neither hear me nor see me?"

Sneezle knelt before her on one knee. "Please, can you help me get home? I must tell our king about these men so he knows what he is fighting."

The faery shook her head sadly. "As long as I inhabit this form, I'm as bound to this place as any house faery. I don't even leave this workshop—how could I get you back to your forest?"

Sneezle heaved an enormous sigh that seemed to rise from the depths of his soul. "But I *have* to get back," he whispered. Every hour away from the hawthorn trees made his heart hang heavier. He blinked back sudden tears.

The golden woman leaned forward to stroke the forest faery's brow. "Don't give up hope, little man. There's someone else you must talk to. A faery who is wiser than I. Perhaps he'll be able to help you."

"Lady, now where must I go?"

"To see the Old One," she advised.

"And where is he?"

"At the very top of the grandfather clock standing in the hall." Aurora untied a bell from her golden braids and placed it in his palm. "Take this, little man. It's magic, of course. Use it when you need it most. Now go, and quickly, Sneezle, for the hour is growing late."

Go? But he had questions still. "First, can you tell me—" he began.

But the woman before him was only a doll, one finger held up to her lips. The other dolls had frozen, too, posed differently than they'd been before. Violet still blew a kiss, but she was immovable now.

Sneezle made another low bow to Aurora and whispered, "Thank you, Lady." Then he pocketed her bell and climbed down from the tabletop. Taking hold of Courage, he crawled back to the hidden corridors. To his surprise, the rat soldiers were still there waiting for him.

"Where to next?" said a rat faery with a big black patch over one eye.

"To the grandfather clock."

"Righty-o," said the soldier, giving Sneezle a smart salute.

They reached the clock without mishap, and the soldiers lifted him up to it, standing one upon another to boost Sneezle high enough. A chain dangled down the clock's center and a long brass arm swung back and forth. The boy grabbed hold of the chain and climbed, ducking each time the arm passed by, hauling himself up and up with effort, and finally reached the top.

He squeezed himself past levers and gears and found himself in an upper room where large brass wheels turned in a steady rhythm, clicking and clacking. In the very center of the room, lit by the light of a fat candle, was a high wood stool—upon which sat a house brownie, fast asleep. The Old One was very old indeed, with wisps of hair turned white as snow beneath the brown peaked cap that marked him as a sorcerer.

"Sir?" said Sneezle.

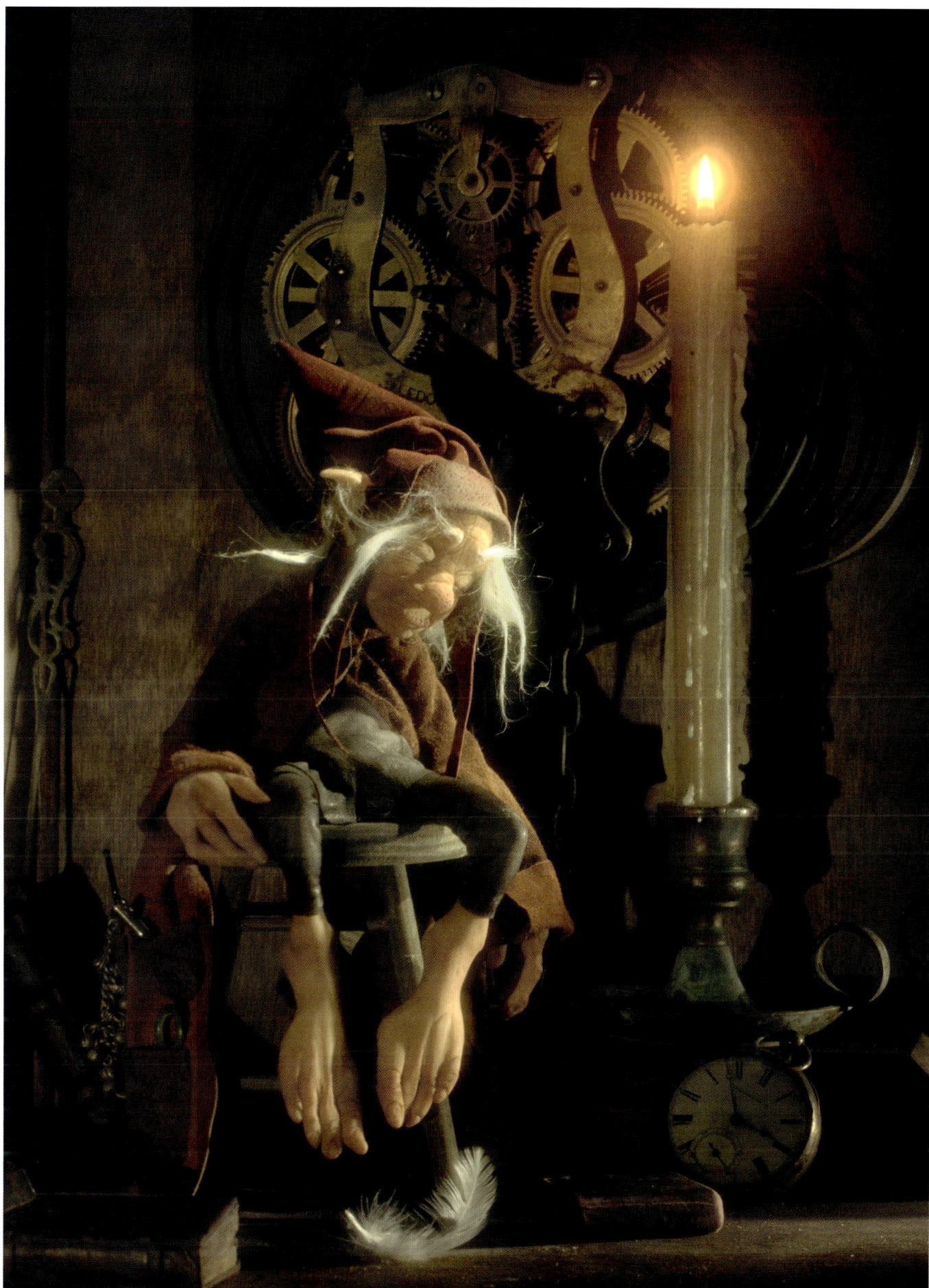

The Old One snored.

"SIR!"

The Old One's eyebrows twitched.

"HEY YOU! OLD ONE! WAKE UP!" the boy shouted. Then he felt a little abashed, for Sneezle had been raised to treat his elders with respect.

Below, the clock began to strike. *One, two, three, four.*

He clapped his hands over his ears as the sound echoed through the chamber.

Five, six, seven, eight.

The Old One shuddered, and his eyes opened. "Ey? What's that? Who goes there?" he said, peering blearily around him.

"It's just me, sir. My name is Sneezle."

"Come closer, boy," the Old One said, "for my eyes aren't what they used to be."

Sneezle came forward and saw that the wizened brownie was almost blind.

The Old One put a hand out to Sneezle's face, touching his ears and cheeks. Then his face wrinkled into a smile. "A root faery! That's a surprise!"

"I'm sorry for waking you up, sir," said the boy.

"Waking me up? Why, I never sleep! Time stops for no man, and no faery either. It's my job to keep this clock going, young man. I never rest." But the Old One's eyes were drifting closed once more.

"Wait, sir, please, don't go back to sleep!"

But the Old One was already snoring. Sneezle grabbed a nearby wrench and banged loudly on the metal clockworks.

"Ey? What's that? Who goes there?"

"It's Sneezle, sir, and I need your help."

"Sneezle! How pleasant to see you again! You've become quite the regular visitor, boy. Very kind of you, for my vigilance here can be tedious."

"Aurora sent me," said Sneezle, and he told the old brownie his story. "Aurora said you could help me to get home to Old Oak Wood," he finished.

"Why, bless me, boy. What use am I? Haven't performed a spell in years. Oh dear. Don't look so sad. Perhaps there's something useful in my book. Now, where did I put my spell book? Memory's not what it used to be." He patted his pockets, emptying them of nuts and bolts, an oddly shaped tool, an apple, a lightbulb, a dainty glass slipper. At last a book of spells appeared, seeming much too large and thick for the pocket it had come from. The brownie handed it to Sneezle. "My eyes aren't what they used to be, son."

"I'll help you, sir," said Sneezle, "if you tell me what I'm looking for."

"Hmmm. Now let me think," he murmured. He sat and he thought for such a long time that Sneezle was certain he'd fallen asleep, until the brownie stabbed the air with his finger. "Page sixty-three!"

Sneezle flipped quickly through the book until he found the page. "An Ointment for Faery Sight," he read. "I think you've got the wrong spell, sir."

"Oh no, Sneezle, that's the one that you want."

"It is?" asked Sneezle dubiously.

"It is!" the old brownie insisted. "You must go and make this ointment, boy, then put it into Rowan's eyes. She's the one who makes the stick men, and she's the one whose aid you need. Talk to her! But first you are going to have to make her see you."

Sneezle shuddered. Talk to a human? But human beings were just so . . . big. He looked down at the book of spells. The recipe was complicated: dandelion seeds gathered in a brass cup, the juice of a toadstool with only six spots, a pinch of earth where maidens had danced, watercress gathered by witches in white . . . the list went on and on. "Where will I get all of these things?"

"The mistress will get them for you, of course. So run along, boy, and ask her for them." The brownie was starting to yawn again, his good eye closing.

"But the mistress is gone!" Sneezle protested.

"Gone? The mistress?" The Old One blinked. "Oh yes, of course she is gone. Silly me. My memory isn't quite—"

"—what it used to be." Sneezle sighed as he put the spell book down, disappointment mixed with relief. He didn't want to talk to humans. But now how would he get home?

"So sorry, my boy," the Old One was saying. He seemed to be drifting off once more. "Spell book is useless . . . now that the mistress . . ." His head slumped forward on his chest. "Pity . . . no other magic here . . . mandrake root . . . or elder twigs . . ."

"ELDER TWIGS!" cried Sneezle so loudly that the old brownie's eyes flew open again. "Elder twigs! I've got elder twigs!" He pulled them out of his waistcoat pocket.

The Old One peered through his one good eye. "Twigs from the very top of the tree? Freely given by a bona fide dryad?" He slowly tottered to his feet and took the small twigs in his palm. A smile creased his wrinkled face. "My word, but these are beauties!"

They looked unremarkable to Sneezle, but the brownie handled them reverently. He cupped the twigs in one large hand and patted his coat pockets with the other, pulling out a small glass vial, a fish, and a mortar and pestle.

"Take these, Sneezle. Not the fish. Now grind the twigs into a fine powder. And as you work, think of your woods. Put your love for it into the magic."

Sneezle placed the twigs in the mortar, grinding awkwardly with the pestle. The twigs merely splintered, and Sneezle frowned. They'd never turn into powder! But he followed the old brownie's instructions and thought of his forest as he worked—his home, his glen, his hawthorn trees, the scent of rain and woodland earth. And as he worked, the twigs transformed into a powder, light and fine, sparkling with pale green lights and smelling just like the forest.

"Excellent, excellent," murmured the Old One, propped up by his crooked cane.

Sneezle poked at the green powder. "What should I do with this?"

"A pinch in her eyes," said the Old One, drifting. "Just a pinch . . . a pinch will do. . . ."

"How?" Sneezle asked him urgently.

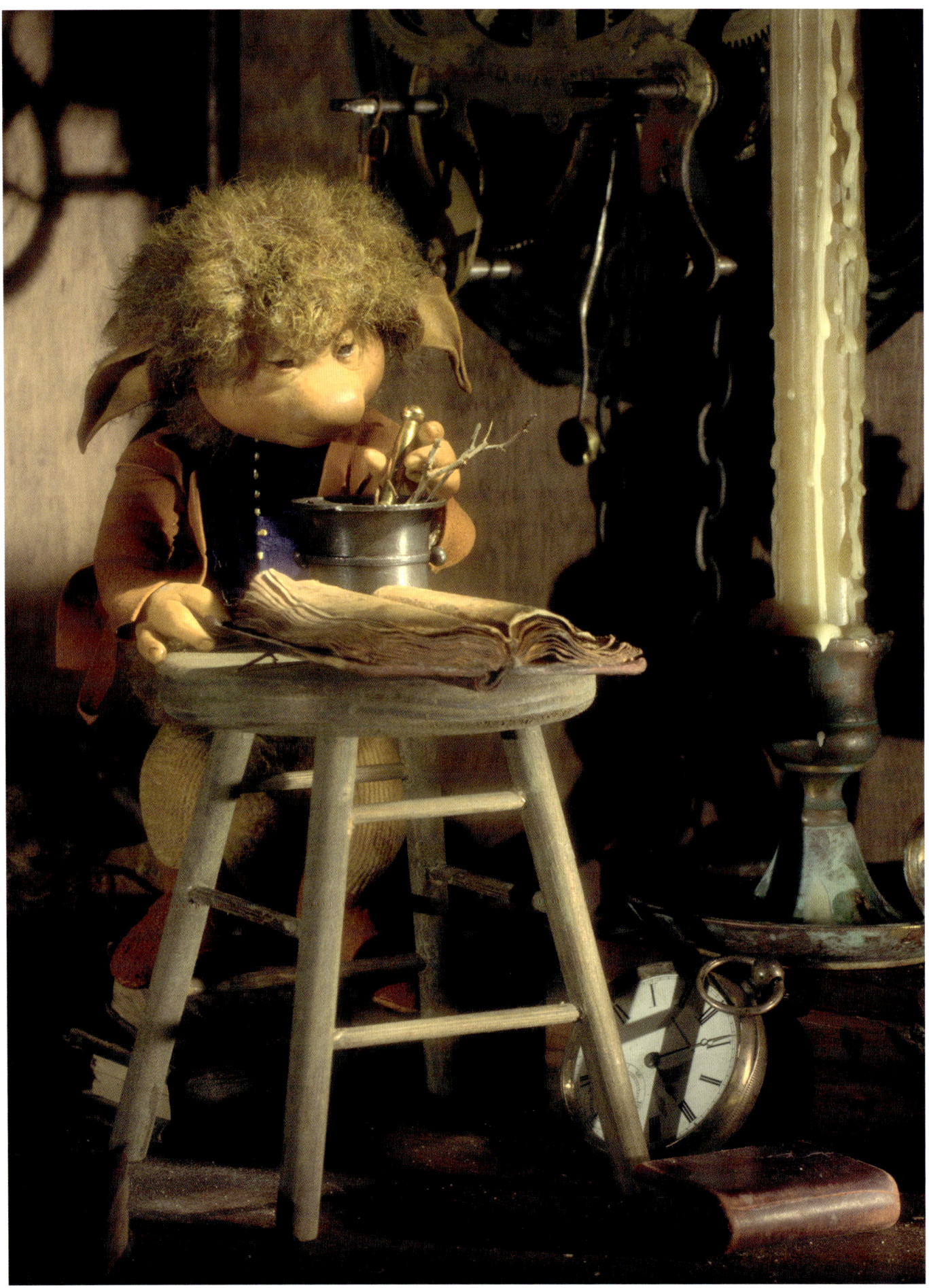

But the Old One was asleep. His snores filled up the small chamber, and now Sneezle could not wake him. The root faery sighed, picked up a vial, and poured the green powder into it. Then he tucked the vial into his pocket and climbed down from the clock.

Sneezle retraced his steps through the cottage walls until he reached the parlor, where he said farewell to the rat soldiers at the hole by the foot of the wardrobe. He climbed the wardrobe—then looked down to see Rowan in the room below, stretched out on the sofa with the black cat curled beside her.

She seemed to be sleeping. As he watched, the girl's mother entered the room, touched Rowan on the shoulder, and said, "Come, darling. It's time for bed."

Rowan opened her eyes slowly. "I'm comfortable, Mum. Can I stay down here?"

"Now, Rowan, no arguments tonight. You have a lovely bedroom upstairs. You always used to like sleeping there."

"But I can hear noises under the bed!"

"Don't be silly," said her mother. "Darling, you're just imagining things."

"Please, Mum," the girl pleaded, "let me sleep on the couch tonight. Or else let me come sleep with you. Don't send me to that room!"

"Rowan," her mother snapped, "I'm tired of hearing about faeries, and funny noises, and monsters under the bed! You're too old for such nonsense. Go upstairs and go to sleep, young lady!"

"Yes, Mum," sighed Rowan, rising from the couch. Sneezle could see her trembling. As she left the room, he crossed the wardrobe and knocked on Billy's door.

The door swung open and Billy cried, "Delightful to see you again, young sir! What news do you bring? Has your quest been successful?"

"I have much to tell you," said Sneezle.

"Come in and share my supper, then. You must be famished," the brownie replied.

He led the way to a dining hall, where he laid another place setting and pulled a second chair up to an old oak dining table. Sneezle *was* famished. He barely spoke a word until their supper was done, but when his host broke out the port, he recounted his adventures.

Billy listened to Sneezle, amazed. "Gracious, you've met rat royalty! And Aurora! And the Old One, too! He is a legend among our kind. Come, what advice did he give you?"

Sneezle gulped. "That I'm to ask Rowan for help."

"Rowan?" said Billy, puzzled. "What help can the human girl be? She doesn't even see us faeries."

Sneezle pulled the vial from his pocket and handed it to Billy. "The Old One says to put this in her eyes. And then she will."

The brownie stared at him, mouth open. It took a moment before he could speak. "Oh think, Sneezle! Think what this could mean, if Rowan could actually learn to see us! She'd help you get back to your woods. She'd stop making those little men. She'd learn to be the mistress here, and there wouldn't be any more boggarts!" The brownie stopped, his voice choked up, and then he added quietly, "And I would no longer be in danger of turning into a boggart myself."

Sneezle felt ashamed. He hadn't thought about what this could mean to Billy; all that he'd been thinking about was getting back to the forest. But could he do it? Was he actually brave enough to talk to a Big Person? The very idea made his knees go weak, and at last he admitted this.

Billy looked at Sneezle with sympathy. "I wish I could help you, friend. But you are the one who made the powder—it's your magic, and you must use it. Yet, Sneezle, if this task should prove too great, no one will blame you for it. You'll always have a home here in my house should you ever need it."

Sneezle gazed back at the kind brownie and silently vowed to conquer his fear—for Billy's sake, as well as his own . . . and for all the faeries of house and wood. He took a breath, leaned forward, and said, "You *can* help, Billy, if you're willing. I think that I may have a plan. . . ."

"I'm willing!" said the brownie, and listened.

At midnight, the two companions set the plan in motion. The clock in the hall struck twelve as they perched on top of the wardrobe, Dinah prowling in the dark below.

"Ready?" Sneezle asked his friend.

"Ready," Billy Blind answered.

The root faery put two fingers in his mouth, and then he whistled three times. And at this signal, the entire rat faery army poured into the parlor.

Dinah whirled around, growling.

The rat princess was leading the charge, formations of soldiers lined up behind her, their fighting sticks held high.

Dinah backed away in confusion. Faeries were supposed to run, not attack! The faery army surrounded the cat, fighting sticks whirling, holding her back, while Sneezle and Billy climbed down and ran past them all and up the stairs.

"Quick!" said Sneezle, panting. "I don't know how much longer those soldiers can hold her!"

"This way to Rowan's bedroom," said the house brownie as he took the lead.

They crossed a landing, ran through a door, and found themselves in a moonlit room filled with toys and books, a carved oak bed at the center of it.

"Go up the drapes!" Sneezle directed, "up over that shelf, out of Dinah's reach!"

They could hear a commotion downstairs, and the rat princess yelling, "Don't let her go!"

They clambered to the top of the tall bookshelf, then peered over the edge—and gasped, for the room was filled with strange blue lights whizzing madly about. The lights were held by grinning, gloating faeries with clawed fingers and toes. "Boggarts!" cried Billy. Dozens and dozens of them, whirling out of control.

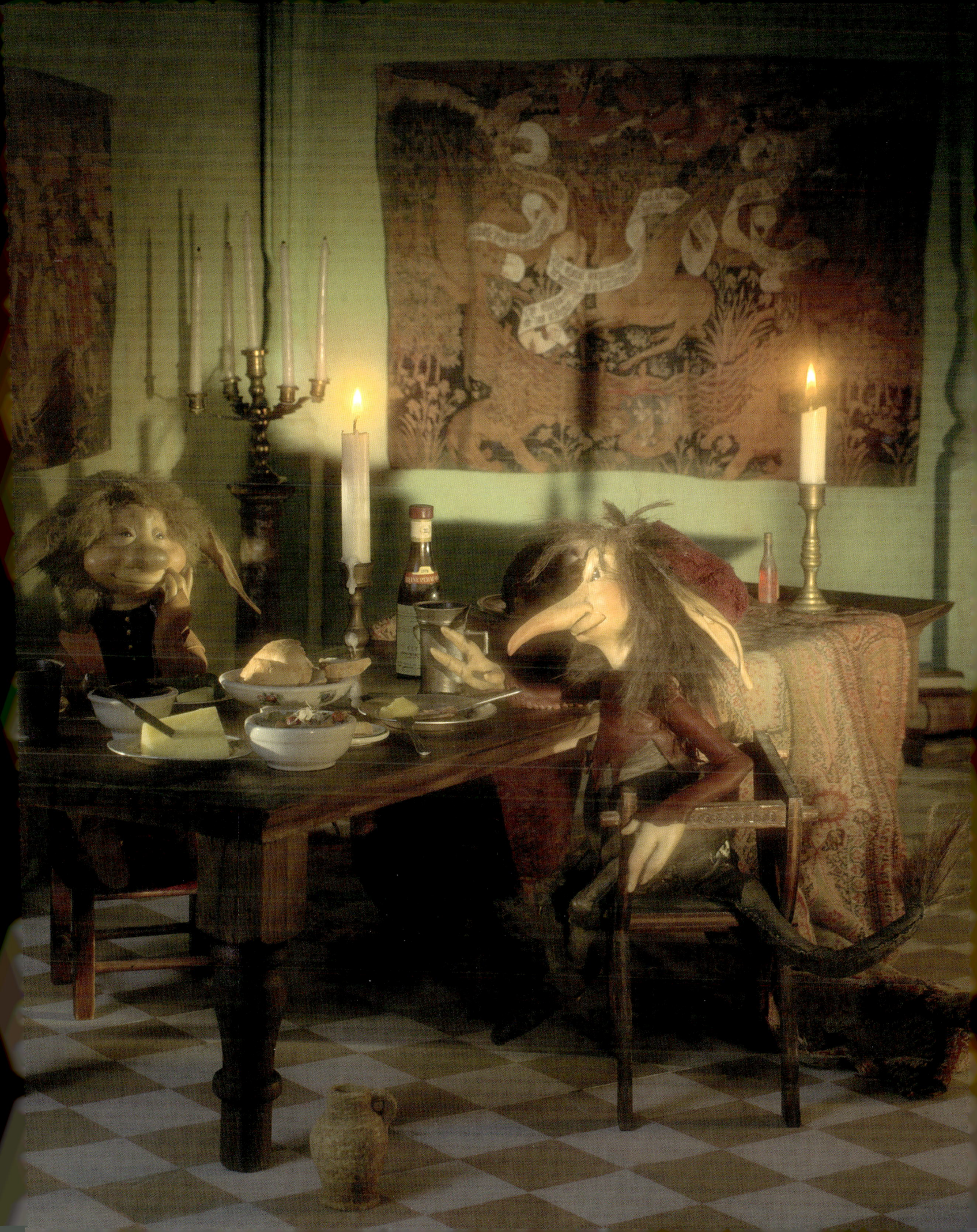

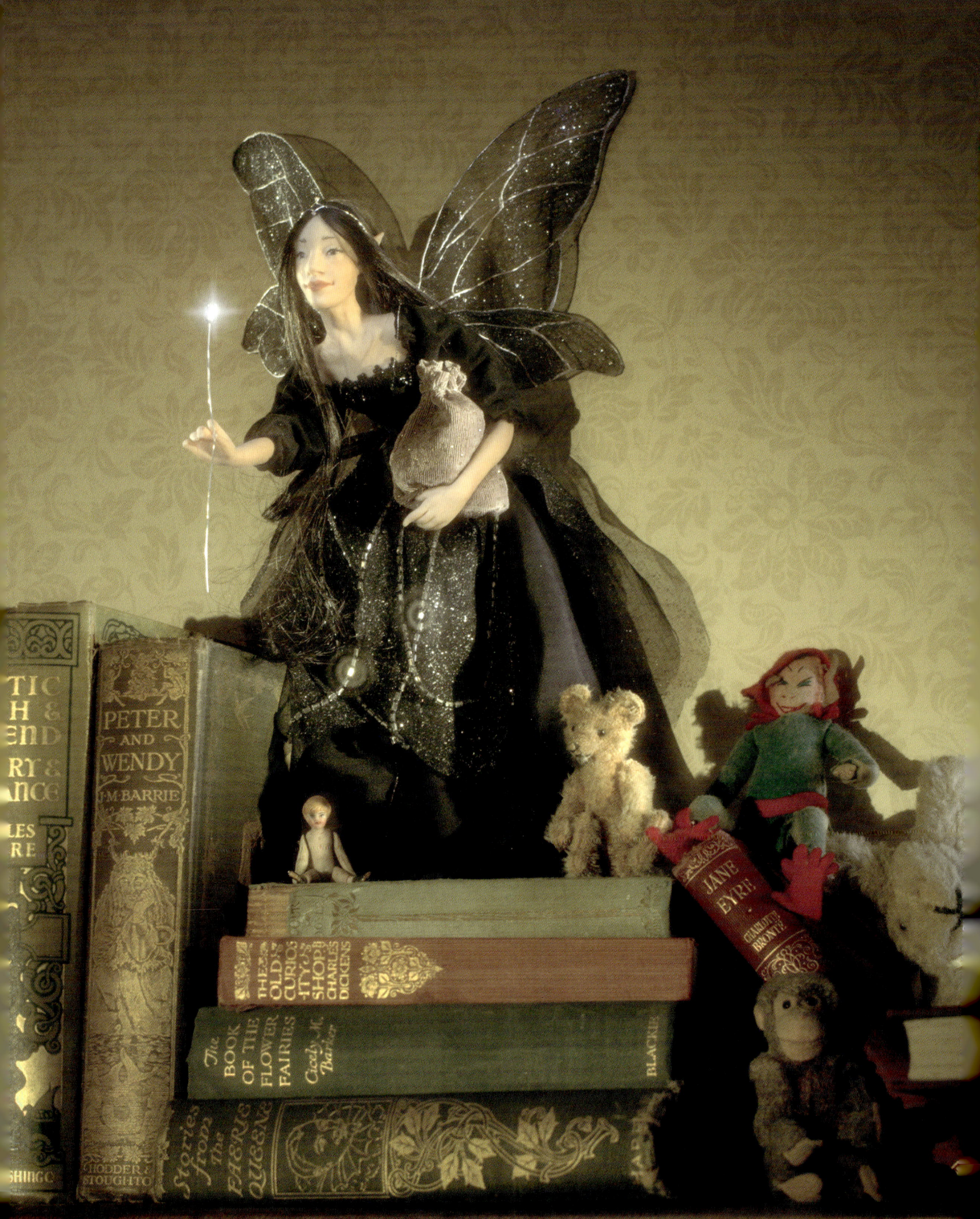

The boggarts seemed to be everywhere. One was stealing socks from a drawer, another dribbled ink on a book, and another was nibbling tiny holes in Rowan's woolly sweaters. From underneath the big wood bed came a growling sound worse than all the rest, while Rowan lay stiff and wide-awake, looking terrified.

"She sees them!" said Sneezle.

"No, but she hears them. At night, in the dark," said a voice from above.

The voice belonged to a slender faery with wings made from the light of stars. Her dress sparkled, and she held a long silver wand and a spangled sack.

"I know you," said the house brownie. "You're Glitter, Rowan's guardian faery. You're the one who guards her sleep and puts dream dust in her eyes."

"And a difficult job it is, too!" snapped Glitter. "That child barely sleeps anymore! If someone doesn't do something about these boggarts soon, I'm leaving!"

"That's exactly what we're here to do," said Sneezle, clutching the vial of powder. "Glitter, how do you get close to her eyes with all these boggarts around?"

"I rap them firmly on the head with my wand," she said. "They don't scare *me*."

"Will you help me to get close to her?" asked Sneezle.

"What's in it for me if I do?"

"What do you mean what's in it for you? You're her guardian faery! You're supposed to help!"

"Oh, I suppose," said Glitter, pouting. "But you're the one asking for a boon, and that means that you owe me something."

"All right," said Sneezle reluctantly, "I'll give you my magical golden bell."

Glitter turned up her nose. "I don't like gold. I only like silver."

"But I haven't got any silver!" he cried. "No, wait, I do have a silver ring." He fished into his pocket and found the ring from the cabinet knight's armor. He tossed it up to the hovering faery, who caught it and looked it over.

"That's not a ring, it's a bracelet, you goose."

"Then give it back!"

"Oh, no, I'll take it! I'll fly you over to Rowan's bed, but then you're on your own."

The guardian faery fluttered down, took hold of Sneezle under his arms, then beat her wings and swooped over toward the bed as he dangled below. It was a stomach-turning ride, looping up and down the room as they dodged the boggarts—who shrieked and hollered and stuck out long tongues at them. Glitter batted them with her wand as she cleared a pathway to the bed, and then she let go of the boy, who tumbled to the pillows. As he picked himself up, rubbing his bottom, he could hear her giggling above. Then he turned and found Rowan beside him, blankets drawn to her chin.

Rowan's eyes were open wide, yet she did not see the forest faery tiptoeing through the long strands of her hair spread across the pillow. Sneezle drew closer and closer, his heart in his throat, his knees shaking. He took a pinch of elder powder and leaned closer . . . and closer still . . . just as the cat burst through the door and leapt onto the bed.

Glitter shrieked and darted to the ceiling. Sneezle clutched his vial and ran, bolting over the quilts as quickly as his feet could run. But Dinah proved to be quicker still, snagging his waistcoat with one sharp claw. He could not rip free. Sneezle shut his eyes. Her breath was hot upon his fur. And then he felt a scratchy tongue lick his cheeks . . . and his ears . . . and his belly. . . .

"Hey, hey, that tickles!" Sneezle gasped, laughing, his face flushed red. Dinah gave him one last lick and, purring, let him go. The forest faery stared up at the cat, astonished. So *that's* what he'd been afraid of? All that growling, all that chasing . . . the cat had only wanted to play!

Dinah stared calmly back at him as she settled herself at Rowan's feet, purring loudly, casually grooming herself with a long pink tongue.

Sneezle took a breath and jumped back to his feet with new resolution. He would do what he'd come here to do, and stop listening to foolish fears. The faery marched right over the quilts, past the lump of the human girl's toes, her knees, her hips, and then he reached her shoulder, the powder in his hand.

But then the bed began to shake. Boggarts whizzed in the air above, hooting, teasing whatever it was that growled so horribly below. The boggarts hooted louder and louder. The growling grew into a roar. Rowan gasped, sat up, turned on the light, and Sneezle went flying.

He somersaulted over the blankets and finally landed on his back, wedged between the bed and a small oak table that stood beside it.

"Dinah, did you hear that?" said Rowan. "Oh, it sounded horrible! I'm not going to sleep, and I'm not turning off this light, no matter what Mum says!"

Sneezle gingerly picked himself up. What on earth was he going to do now? How could he put the powder in Rowan's eyes if she didn't lie down? The girl was reaching over him for a glass of water on the bedside table, and quick as thought, he put a pinch of powder into the glass.

Sneezle watched as the girl took a little sip, and then another one. But the water looked exactly the same—there was no green spark of magic in it. He sat down on the mattress, sighing. This simply wasn't going to work.

Rowan put the glass back down and rubbed her blue eyes wearily. And then she blinked. And stared at the small brown faery on the bed beside her.

"Oh, my," she whispered.

Sneezle got up and took a cautious step toward her.

"Look, Dinah, look! It moved!"

"I'm not an *it*, I am a *he*," said Sneezle.

"A he?" said the girl, her eyes as wide as saucers. "Are you a faery, then?"

"Of course I am!" Sneezle replied.

"A real faery," breathed Rowan in wonder.

"That's right. A faery. And real as dirt. My name is Sneezlewort," he told her, approaching ever closer as his heart pounded in his chest.

"S-s-sneezlewort?" the girl repeated, stuttering a little, just like he did, and suddenly Sneezle wasn't so scared. He gave her a tentative smile.

The human smiled at him with a smile as shy as any faery's. "S-s-so you're the thing that's been living underneath my bed?" she asked him anxiously.

"Certainly not!" the young faery told her. "You've got a boggart under your bed!"

"A boggart!"

Sneezle nodded at her. "In fact, this house is infested with them—especially this room."

"I knew it!" said Rowan. "Mum said it was mice!"

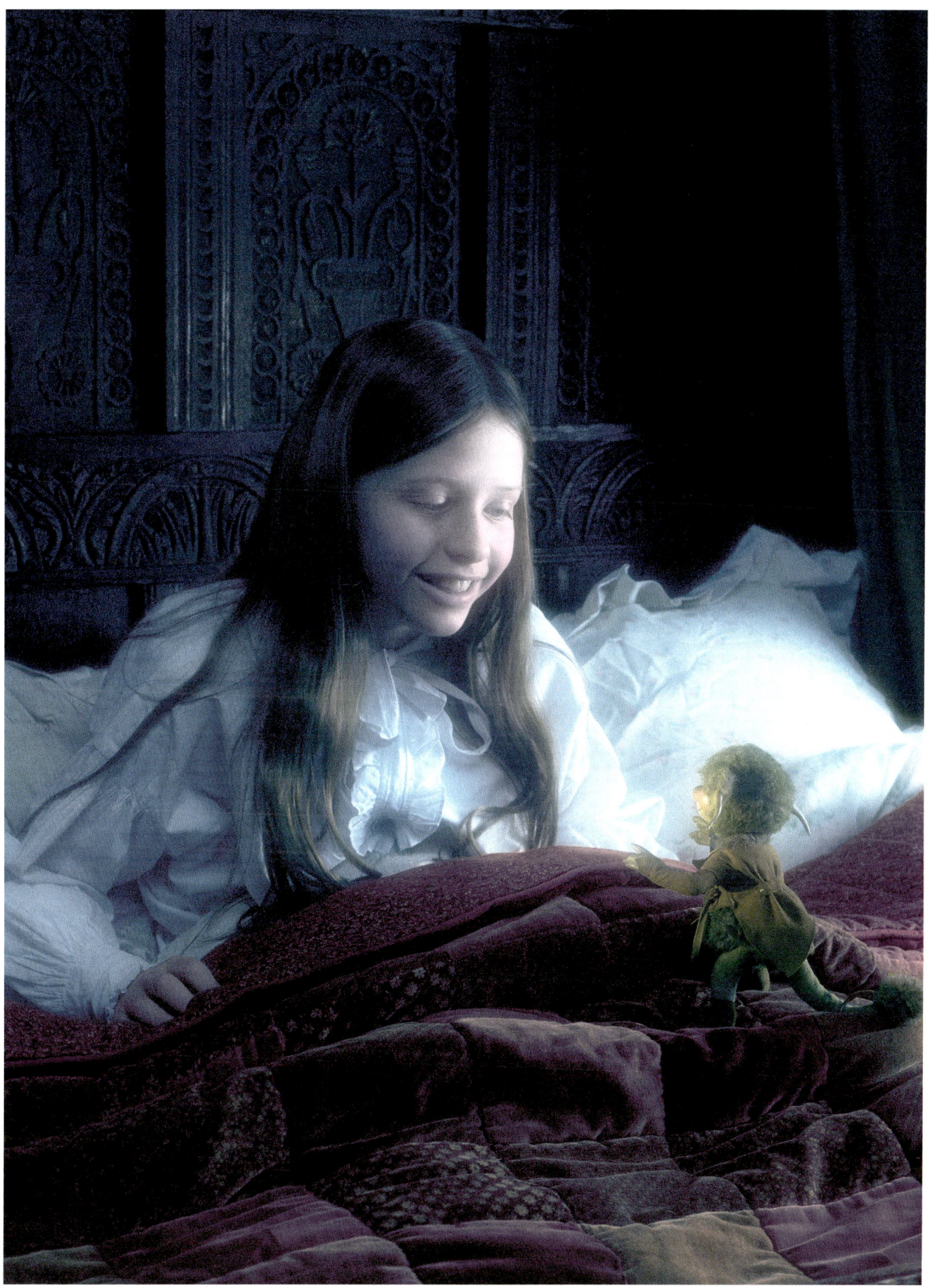

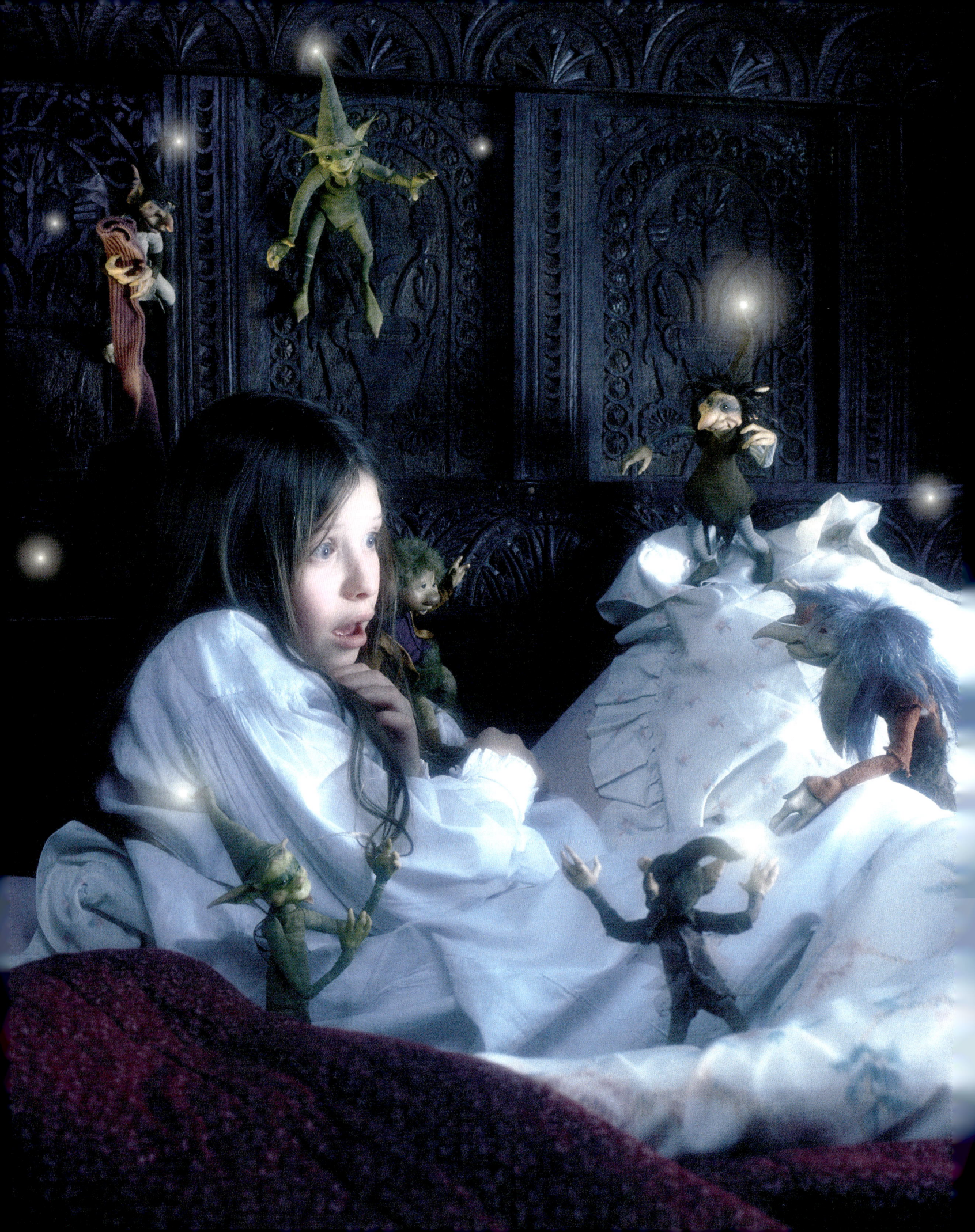

"That's only because she can't see faeries."

"My grandmother can," said Rowan proudly.

Sneezle sat on the pillow beside her. "Your grandmother was the mistress here, looking after all the house faeries. Now that she's gone, Rowan, you're going to have to take her place."

"I can't!" cried Rowan.

"Why not?" he asked.

"It's just . . . I'm not like my grandmother. Grandma's good at everything. Not me. I can't do magic, I can't make dolls, I only pretend to see faeries. Grandma thought I could really see them—and she told me to look after them. When she comes back, she'll see that I didn't. She'll be so disappointed!"

"But you *do* see faeries. You're seeing one now."

"I'm probably just dreaming," said Rowan stubbornly.

"Do you think so? Then turn off the light."

"The light?"

"Go on."

Rowan switched it off. The boggarts returned, whizzing and whirling and spinning around the young girl's head. She shrieked and turned the light back on. "Oh my gosh, *those* are the boggarts?"

"They are indeed," said Sneezle gravely, "and you've got to help us get rid of them." He called Billy and Glitter down and introduced the faeries to Rowan. And then he recounted the whole of his story, while the human girl listened, enthralled.

"I'm sorry I made those stick men," she said. "I promise that I won't make any more! I want to help you with the boggarts, but what if I make it worse?"

"You won't," said Billy.

"She might!" said Glitter.

"You have to try your best," said Sneezle. "Lady Aurora told me that you have magic, and she would know."

"You are the mistress here," said Billy, "at least until your grandmother returns. So *you* must order the boggarts to leave. You must tell them they're not welcome here—not unless they turn back into the brownies they were before."

"But what if the boggarts don't listen to me?"

"You must make them listen," said Billy firmly, "as only the mistress of Spring Cottage can."

Rowan frowned. "Perhaps we'd better just wait until Grandma comes back."

"But that could be too late for me," the house brownie reminded her gently.

The girl swallowed, her face grown pale. "You're right. I'm sorry. I'll try." Sneezle touched her hand softly, for he knew what it felt like to be afraid, and Rowan gave him a grateful look. She said, "Will you three stay with me?"

"Of course we will," Billy replied.

"We'll be right here beside you," said Sneezle.

He glared at Glitter until she muttered, "Oh, all right. I'll stay."

Rowan took a steadying breath. "Okay then, faeries, here I go. Wish me luck." She leaned over to the light, and switched it off.

As soon as she did, the boggarts returned, whizzing from wall, to wall, to wall. Rowan began to tremble, and the more she did, the wilder they grew.

Sneezle dashed up to her shoulder. "Go on, Rowan. Do it now!"

He clung tightly to Rowan's hair as the girl rose and stood on the bed. "Okay, boggarts," she said loudly. "I've had enough! You have to leave! I want you to go right now, you hear? You're no longer welcome in Spring Cottage—not unless you turn into nice little brownies. Boggarts, are you listening? We don't want you here, get out!"

The wild boys screeched to a halt and stared at the girl on the bed, dumbfounded. First they laughed in disbelief . . . until they found they were starting to shrink. Their lights began to flicker and dim. And then the boggarts started to flee, streaming out of every cottage window, flooding the night beyond . . . except for a few, who turned back to brownies, blinking and looking confused.

But one big boggart stood his ground, shaking an angry fist at her. "You'll not be rid of me!" he growled, a stolen sock under his arm.

"Leave! Depart! Get out of here! Scram!" Rowan said, pointing firmly at the door.

The big boggart just sneered at her. "What will you give me if I do?"

"What do you want?" she asked, suspicious.

"How about your little finger?" he smirked.

"Ew, gross. No way!"

"Your toe?"

"Forget it!"

"Your mother, then," the boggart said. "She doesn't love you. GIVE HER TO ME."

"You're lying. Of course my mother loves me! Okay, she's a little bossy sometimes. But I love her anyway and you can't have her. So just get lost!"

"You won't bargain? So then I'll stay," the boggart smirked.

Sneezle took out his golden bell. "Try this," he urged in Rowan's ear.

"What's that? What's that? Whatever it is, I want it!" the greedy boggart cried.

Rowan took the little bell from Sneezle. "You can have it on one condition. You have to promise you'll never come back and do mischief again."

"All right, it's a deal," the boggart growled, mesmerized by Aurora's sparkling bell. "Just give that pretty-pretty to me and do it quick!" he roared.

She tossed the bell and he snatched it up. Then his gloating face began to contort. A golden glow traveled from the bell and up his fingers, up his arm. The light entirely filled him, from the tips of his toes to the top of his head. With a hissing sound, like air out of a tire, he started to shrink in size . . . and as he did, he turned back into a brownie, colored brilliant gold.

Billy grinned. "Well done, young miss!"

But then they heard a terrible roar. The creature under the bed was still there, and sounding more ferocious than ever.

"Why didn't that boggart leave with the others?" cried Rowan, backing away from the sound.

"Maybe it isn't a boggart after all!" said Billy Blind, alarmed

"But what should I do?" cried Rowan. She'd been terrified of this creature for weeks.

Sneezle gulped and shook his head. "Perhaps we'd all better run!"

"No," said Rowan suddenly. "I'm tired of being so scared, Sneezle. I'm going to face it down!"

"Don't do it! Don't do it!" cried Glitter. "The boy is right. Just run!"

But Rowan had already stepped down from her bed. She knelt upon the rug, peered into the dark below the bed . . . and began to laugh.

She reached under the bed and brought a tiny faery out in her palm. A tiny, tiny faery with huge brown eyes, trembling like a leaf.

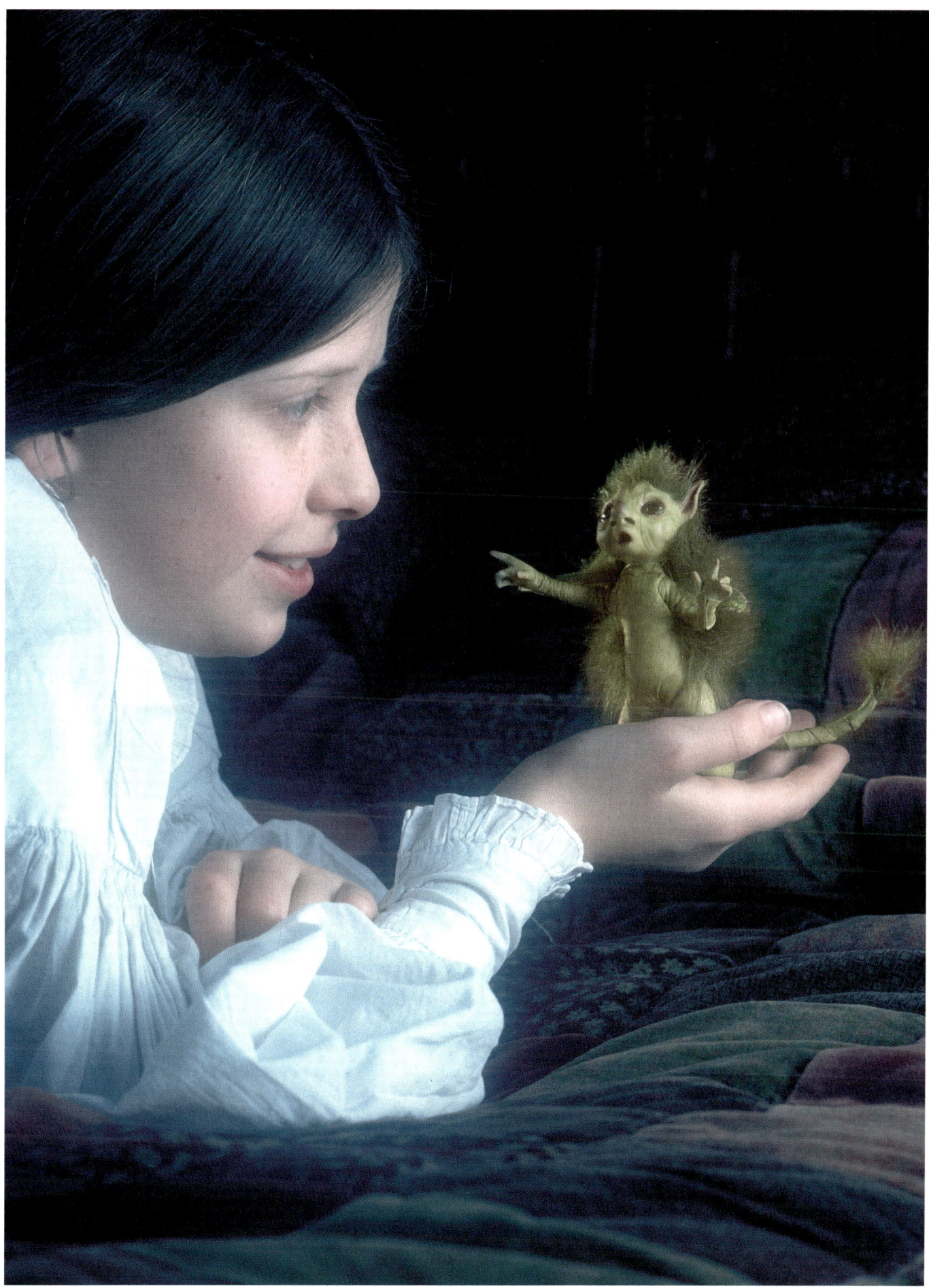

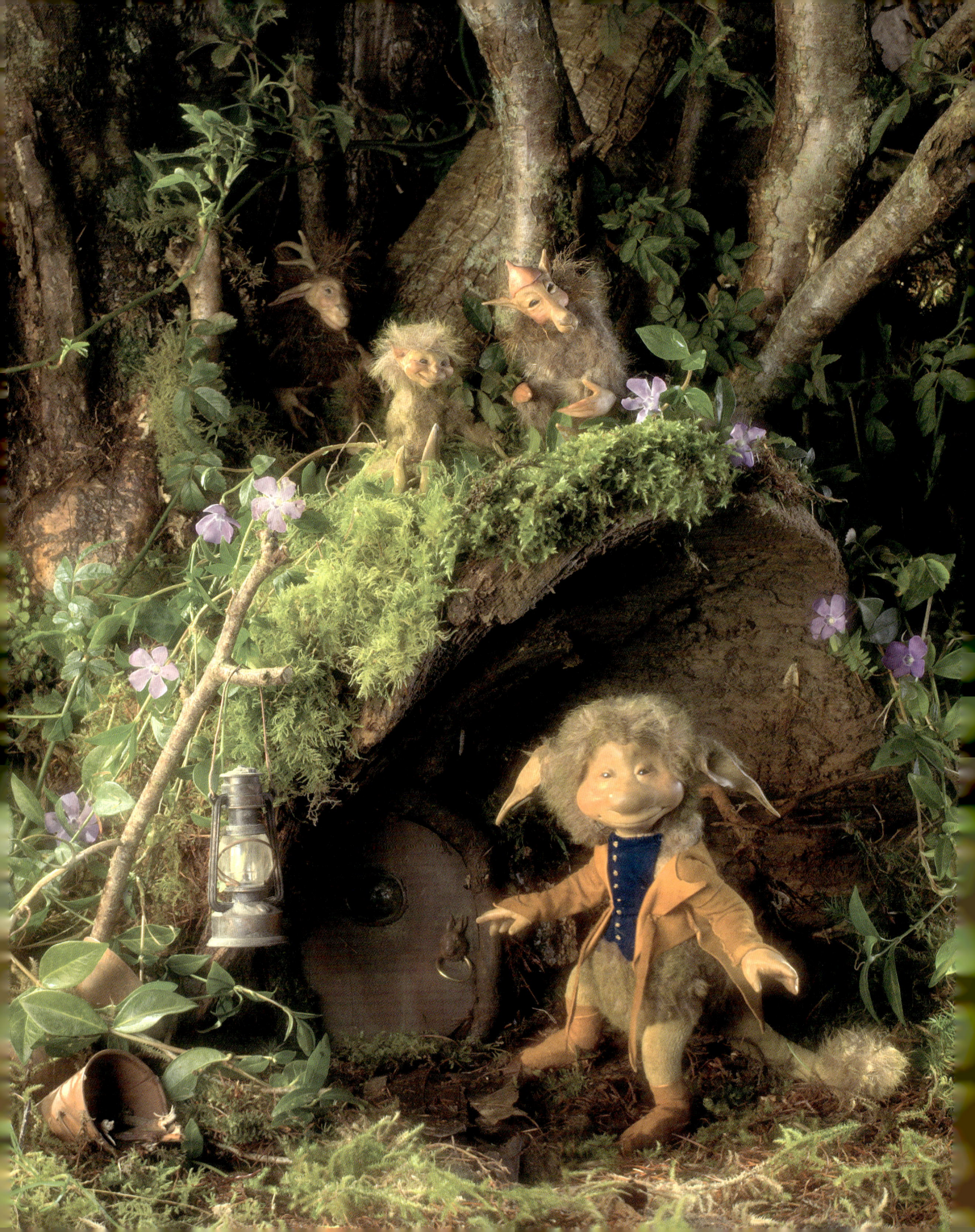

"It was just you, all this time!"

The little faery whispered back, "I was scared of those mean boggarts. Please, miss, are the boggarts gone?"

"They are," Rowan assured the tiny creature.

He heaved a sigh of relief. "Then please, miss, can I have some milk and toast? My tummy is growling."

"Everyone shall have milk and toast, every faery in this house," Rowan promised.

The faery cuddled shyly against her hand. "Are you the new mistress?"

Rowan hesitated, and then she smiled. "Why yes, I guess I am—until my grandmother comes back."

"And then we'll have *two* mistresses," said Billy Blind, quite overcome, wiping the tears that sprang to his eyes with the end of his tufted tail.

When Sneezle left his beloved woods, he never, ever could have imagined that when he finally returned, it would be riding on a human's shoulder. A winding path crossed over the moor from Spring Cottage to the forest's edge, then led through the woods to a ring of oaks, where Rowan set him down. A green light filtered through the trees as he breathed the scents of water and earth. Sneezle was home at last and the oak trees rustled to welcome him back.

Rowan gave the faery a wistful look. "Shall I ever see you again?"

"I could visit you," said Sneezle, "if you promise not to make stick men again!"

"I promise. I'll make much better things. And I'll be more careful of what I make."

"You must, Rowan," said Sneezle seriously. "Your magic is very strong."

"Like Grandma's?" she asked, her eyes gleaming.

"Of course not," said the faery. "It's *your* magic. Why should it be like anyone else's? But it's just as good," he added, smiling, and blushed when Rowan kissed him.

He left her then, and made his way to the stream and up to the dryad's pool. He had used up all the elder, and he still needed some for Twig. The sun was high when he reached the dryad's door beneath the elder roots. He knocked on the door, and knocked again, until the dryad finally answered.

"Ah, so it's you, small one. You're back again. Have you a story for me?"

"I do, Lady," said Sneezle, grinning broadly. "I do indeed."

The End

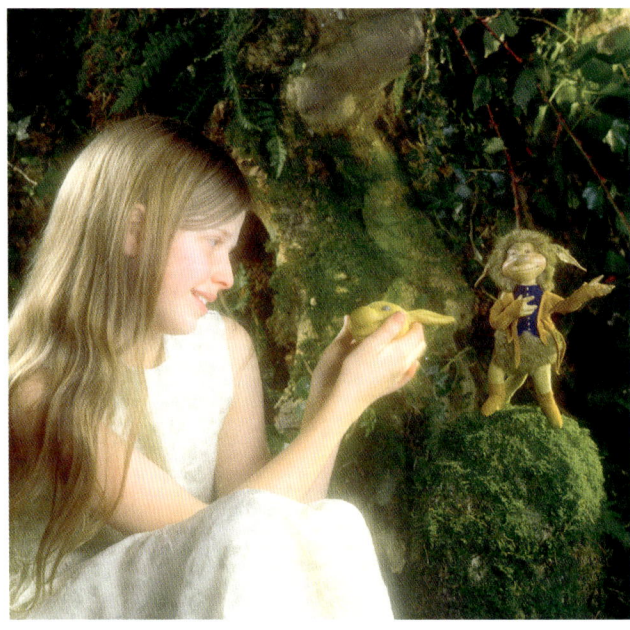

ABOUT THE ARTIST AND AUTHOR

WENDY FROUD became a doll maker at the age of five and has gone on to make dolls, puppets, and sculpture for such films as *The Empire Strikes Back*—she is credited as the fabricator of its beloved character Yoda—and Jim Henson's *The Dark Crystal, Labyrinth, The Muppet Show,* and *The Muppet Movie.* Her dolls and figures are highly sought after by private collectors around the world. Froud grew up in Detroit and now resides in Devon, England, on Dartmoor, with her husband, Brian, and their son, Toby.

TERRI WINDLING, a six-time winner of the World Fantasy Award, has been a guiding force in the development of mythic fiction and fantasy literature for more than a decade. A fairy and folklore scholar, she has written mythic fiction for adults and children (winning the Mythopoeic Award for her novel *The Wood Wife*) and published more than twenty-five anthologies. Most recently she edited *The Green Man: Tales from the Mythic Forest* and *My Swan Sister and Other Retold Fairy Tales* with Ellen Datlow. She divides her time between Devon, England, and Tucson, Arizona.

Simon & Schuster
Rockefeller Center
1230 Avenue of the Americas
New York, NY 10020

This book is a work of fiction. Names, characters, places, and incidents either are products of the author's imagination or are used fictitiously. Any resemblance to actual events or locales or persons, living or dead, is entirely coincidental.

Text copyright © 2003 by Terri Windling
Photographs copyright © 2003 by Wendy Froud
Photographs are ™ World of Froud
A World of Froud/Imaginosis Production

All rights reserved, including the right of reproduction in whole or in part in any form.
SIMON & SCHUSTER and colophon are registered trademarks of Simon & Schuster, Inc.
For information regarding special discounts for bulk purchases, please contact Simon & Schuster Special Sales at 1-800-456-6798 or business@simonandschuster.com

Designed by Wherefore Art?
Manufactured in England

1 3 5 7 9 10 8 6 4 2

Library of Congress Cataloging-in-Publication Data
Windling, Terri.
The faeries of Spring Cottage / art by Wendy Froud; story by Terri Windling; photographs by John Lawrence Jones; sets and photographic art direction by Brian Froud.
p. cm.
1. Sneezle (Fictitious character)—Fiction. I. Froud, Wendy, 1954– II. Jones, John Lawrence. III. Title.
PS3573.I5175 F34   2003   813'.54—dc21   2002030458
ISBN 0-7432-0235-X